SARAH M. ANDERSON WRITING AS

MAGGIE CHASE

HER
EBONY

Acknowledgements

I could not have written this book without the generous help of the following people: Melissa Jolly for everything she does, Shae O'Conner and Laura K. Curtis for their support, Tasha Harrison and Mary Dieterich for editing, and Alexandra Haughton for designing the cover.

Dedication

To Beverly Jenkins

Chapter One

1868

"S he *is* lovely, isn't she?"

The sound of the voice—soft and conversational—jolted Miss Minerva Krenshaw back to herself. Shame burned at the back of her neck, but she hid it behind a frown—a frown directed at the beautiful, young colored woman who was one of the Jewels of the local brothel, the Jeweled Ladies. "I am merely making sure that none of my pupils are anywhere near those..."

As Minerva swung around to face the person to whom she was speaking, the word 'whores' died on her tongue because she found herself face to face with none other than the madam of the Jewels herself, Mistress.

Mistress stood in the dry-goods store in Brimstone, Texas, looking comically out of place. She lifted an eyebrow as if to dare Minerva to finish that sentence.

"...Those girls," Minerva finished weakly. She needed to escape this conversation immediately. Her position as the schoolteacher in this town rested on her reputation remaining completely unimpeachable and being seen in conversation with the infamous madam was the quickest way to impeach anyone's reputation—especially a spinster schoolmarm who might have just been caught staring at a soiled dove.

"Miss…Krenshaw, is it?" Mistress said, politeness dripping off every single syllable. "You're the schoolteacher, aren't you?"

Minerva swallowed. "That is correct."

Mistress's eyes swept over Minerva's dyed brown wool dress, buttoned firmly up to her chin. Aside from her face, not a single inch of Minerva's skin showed. Her gloves were worn kid-leather, but they still served. Self-consciously, she tugged her equally threadbare shawl around her shoulders. No one ever looked at her like Mistress was looking at her now. Their eyes always slid over her as if she blended in with the background.

Which, of course, she did. Her braided hair was hidden under a shapeless bonnet. Her face was plain and her eyes the same dull brown as her hair. Her only adornments were her two most prized possessions— her spectacles and the watch fob pinned to her dress. There was nothing about her that caught the eye. No one's eyes had ever caught before.

Except for now. Mistress's leisurely appraisal of Minerva's person was unnerving. The woman was stunningly beautiful. Everywhere Minerva was plain and brown, Mistress sparkled and shined. Underneath the broad brim of her swooping hat—in and of itself a work of art made of peacock feathers and velvet—her hair must have taken two attendants to arrange thusly. Gems glittered at her ears, her neck and her gloved wrists. The expanse of her bosom was smooth as

2

peaches and cream and, for one maddening moment, Minerva actually lifted her hand to see if that skin felt as pretty as it looked. *Everything* about Mistress was designed to catch the eye.

Minerva had never felt so plain in all her life.

Mistress favored her with a warm smile. "I couldn't help but see that you had noticed Miss White," she said, nodding toward the young woman from whom Minerva had been unable to tear her gaze.

Miss White—an ill-fitting name for the young colored woman. Her skin was a soft brown, like coffee with the luxury of cream in it. She was wearing a black dress that could have been demure—if not for the cut of the velvet, the way it draped over and outlined all the curves of her body.

"Her dress," Minerva said stiffly, desperately trying to sound disapproving. "It's indecent." But she had looked—and been caught staring like a lovesick puppy. "I am just making sure that none of my pupils are about to witness such..." Against her will, she glanced back over at Miss White, at the expanse of bosom so very visible, a set of jet stones nestled against her throat. "Indecency."

"Yes," Mistress murmured, looking extraordinarily pleased with herself. "As you said."

Minerva ground her teeth. "And what are you all doing here?" Because in addition to Miss White and Mistress, there were three other soiled doves, all crowded around a young Native woman as the shopkeeper unrolled bolt after bolt of brown and red fabrics. "Such an outing is uncalled for. The children, you know."

Mistress's lips twitched. "I have a new Jewel,

3

Miss Krenshaw." She nodded toward the cluster. "I'm thinking of calling her Sienna Brown."

Minerva scoffed before she could stop herself. "Really, Madam, I had credited you with, if not morals, then at least intelligence."

Mistress arched an eyebrow at Minerva. "Indeed?"

"Sienna is not a gem. It is a color." She watched Miss White drape a length of rust-colored fabric over the Native girl's shoulders. "And it will wash her out."

Mistress followed Minerva's gaze. "But do I dare take fashion advice from the local schoolmarm?"

"I beg your pardon," Minerva said stiffly. "I am dressed appropriately for my station."

Mistress's lips twitched again and Minerva had the distinct feeling she was being mocked. "What do you recommend?"

"I recommend you turn that young lady over to the care of a church," she snapped. "I cannot condone you corrupting another innocent in your mindless pursuit of money." But even as she said it, her eyes turned back to the cluster of doves. The young Native woman was looking shy as Miss White and the others fussed over her.

Upon closer inspection, Minerva saw something else—the dark bruises fading along her jaw, the girl's inability to smile—or even open her mouth. She gasped when she realized that someone had badly beaten the girl.

"Ah, you see?" Mistress said, her voice soft and gentle and seductive. Against her every wish, Minerva's body responded of its own accord. "I am not the one who corrupted that girl. And she would rather die than go back to a church." Minerva swung

4

around in horror to find Mistress looking down at her with as much severity as Minerva had ever seen. "I am merely teaching that girl she is worth something. Something *more*."

"You're putting a price on her body. On her soul." Mistress couldn't really be saying what Minerva thought she was saying—could she?

Mistress gave her a pitying look. "Better to be paid for it than have it taken by force. Yes, if she chooses, she will work on her back for me. But I will give her freedoms she's never thought possible. Prestige. Safety. Security."

Minerva's hot cheeks got even hotter. "Sinners, all of you," was all she could say.

"Indeed," Mistress murmured. "But Miss Brown is not why I sought you out today, Miss Krenshaw."

"Don't call her that." Minerva was beyond snappish right now, but when she was feeling trapped, she always reverted back to snappishness. It was, in large measure, what made her a successful teacher.

"I value your opinion," Mistress all but cooed. She knew that she was winning this conversation with Minerva.

They both did. "Call her…" Her mind spun. "I do not know which tribe she hails from, but some of those tribes to the west—they like that blue stone the color of the sky." She glanced back at the covey of doves and saw that Miss White had her hand on a bolt of robin's-egg blue fabric. "Call her Turquoise Sky and dress her in blues. It's not a gem but it's a stone and it's a far sight better than *brown*."

Mistress's eyes crinkled appreciatively and Minerva had the oddest feeling that she'd pleased the

5

sinner. Odder still was the feeling of pride that she had earned the madam's approval. "You are quite bright."

"You said you did not seek me out for advice on ladies' gowns?" Minerva said, checking the time on her watch fob. The motion dislodged her glasses and she had to resettle them on her nose. "Do be quick, Madam. I cannot afford to stand around and converse with the likes of you all day. It will cost me my position if people draw an association between us."

"And then where would you be?" Mistress agreed. "I have...a girl," she said and, for the first time, Minerva heard a note of concern in her voice.

"You have more than one. And I am not one of them. Nor," she added stiffly, "will I ever be."

Mistress inclined her head in acknowledgement. "To the point, then. I have a girl who cannot read. She is beautiful and graceful and everything a man could desire in an evening—but she cannot *read*," she repeated.

Minerva gasped. She didn't know which was more shocking—that, in these advanced times, children were still allowed to forgo their education or that the madam of the most notorious brothel in all of Texas would have such a care for her 'girls.' "That is most unfortunate," she agreed. "Everyone should read."

"I feel the same. Look at that," she added with something that appeared to be a wink, "something that you and I agree on. I would like for you to teach this girl to read."

Minerva's hand flew to her chest. "I beg your pardon?"

"Let's cut bait, Miss Krenshaw. My girls command top dollar and many of them save their money for the day they can retire from this life. This particular girl is skilled with a needle and would like to one day open her own shop—not here," she hurried to add when Minerva looked at her in surprise. "She'll go farther west. You and I both know that no matter how graceful and lovely her creations are, no matter how well-spoken or mannered she is, Miss White will never survive as a businesswoman on her own if she cannot *read*."

Minerva's mouth opened and shut. She'd…well, she'd always assumed that Mistress kept the girls working until they were all used up and then discarded them to even less-savory establishments of ill repute. A life begun at the Jeweled Ladies only went downhill from there.

But this? This…caring? Because it *was* caring. In a fashion, anyway. Much like rescuing a Native girl from a violent situation—perhaps even from a church!—and giving her safety and freedom was a kind of caring.

Misguided, poorly formed caring. But caring nonetheless.

"I…" Minerva's mouth opened and shut several times, but all she could seem to say was, "I…" She cleared her throat and tried again.

Minerva glanced back at the knot of women a second time to see that Miss White had indeed picked up the bolt of turquoise fabric and was now laying it across the Native girl's shoulders. Beautiful and alluring and talented with a needle. A young woman who had plans and dreams.

Mistress was right. Dreams she would never be able to achieve if she could not read. "I cannot possibly have a whore in my schoolhouse and I cannot possibly be seen coming and going from your brothel. I would lose my position *and* my reputation and, unlike your girls, I know exactly the value of those two things."

A hundred dollars a year to teach the children of Brimstone their letters and numbers. And that included a room in the back of the schoolhouse where Minerva lived, plus a small stipend of foods donated by grateful parents. It was a hardscrabble life, but it was an honest one. She did good work and she would be rewarded for it. If not in this world—and that seemed less likely by the day—then in the afterlife, surely. As long as she could remember herself and her Bible.

"If I could arrange for you to meet in a neutral location, would you consider it?" When Minerva didn't answer right away, Mistress added, "Or is the fact that she is black the reason you refuse?"

"What? No," Minerva said sharply. "I teach several colored children. It has nothing to do with her race and everything to do with *you*. I cannot take your money and her money is yours, is it not?"

"Yet you took Emmeline McCartney's—oh, I beg your pardon, Mrs. Raymond Dupree's—money for new books, did you not?"

"That was different," Minerva snapped, knowing her cheeks were blushing. "That was her husband's money."

Not that long ago, Mayor Dupree had made the dove known as Emerald Green his bride. The town had still not gotten over the scandal of their mayor—a man of fine, upstanding character from a good family— marrying a former whore. And not just any whore, but Emerald Green, the pride of the Jeweled Ladies.

Minerva had always heard that Emerald Green would one day take over the brothel and run it.

But instead she'd remade herself into an honorable woman. She'd paid for new windows in her husband's Methodist church. She'd donated enough money for new readers as well as slates for the children and had enough left over that Minerva had been able to repair the hole in the roof in the outhouse. She had even talked of sponsoring a library—a real, free library, right here in Brimstone.

In other words, Mrs. Dupree had gone from a woman of ill repute to a pillar of the community in less than a year. Minerva had convinced herself that Mrs. Dupree spent her husband's money. The Duprees were quite rich, after all.

Mistress's eyes swept behind Minerva. "You may think about it," she said, completely ignoring Minerva's refusal. Then she gracefully stepped around Minerva and called out in a sing-song voice, "My darlings, I have had a revelation. Turquoise! Turquoise Sky! Mr. Snyder, be a dear and bring us anything you have in this lovely shade of blue for my newest Jewel."

Minerva quickly paid for her packet of needles and left the dry-goods store without the plain linen she'd wanted to fashion a new pair of drawers from. She couldn't think about her underclothes and those women in the same breath. It was unseemly. Improper. And most certainly immoral.

Even as she fled the shop to go back to her schoolhouse and her drab clothes, her eye caught on Miss White, the jet gems at her neck sparkling in the light.

She was *not* tempted. Not by Mistress's offer nor the thought of spending time with Miss White. Minerva had left her home in New York behind years ago to escape this temptation and she would not give into it now. She was too strong. Unlike those Jewels, she valued her reputation far more than a fleeting moment of pleasure.

Still, as she lingered for just a second too long by the window, Mistress was whispering something in Miss White's ear and Miss White looked out through the shop window. She met Minerva's gaze and her whole face lit up. Even though Minerva would not have thought it possible, the young woman got even lovelier.

Surely not. It had to be a trick of the light. Minerva scowled and shook her head before she stomped back to her schoolhouse.

She would not be tricked. Not again.

Never again.

Chapter Two

Abigail Whithall was on her knees in front of a dress form when the soft knock came on her bedroom door. She glanced at the small clock on the dresser. It was early yet—the gentlemen weren't due to show up until four in the afternoon

"Yes?" she said around a mouthful of pins.

The door swung open and Mistress all but floated into the room. Abigail tensed even as she smiled through her nerves. Mistress was a kind woman—far kinder than Mrs. Whithall had been. And there was no comparison between Mistress and Master Dawson. Mistress did not beat Abigail or force her to do anything she did not wish to. Abigail was paid in cash, deposited in a bank account at the First Macon County Bank—hers, all of it. The bank man, Mr. Hobbs, had assured her that no one would take her account away from her.

Be that as it may, Mistress still held power over Abigail and, kind as she was, that power made Abigail nervous. Once, she'd trusted Dawson when he'd promised to help her to get a shop, and the cost had been too high to bear. She couldn't let that happen again.

Oh, how she longed to be free. Really and truly free, not just the kind of paper freedom that Mr. Lincoln had offered up.

11

Still, this was a good stepping-stone. Abigail watched Mistress study the turquoise dress she was pinning. "As always," Mistress said as Abigail climbed to her feet and pulled her work apron off over her head, "your work is exquisite. It puts those creations we used to order from New Orleans to shame."

Abigail bowed her head so Mistress wouldn't see her smile. "Thank you, Mistress."

A slender finger with a long, smooth nail slid under her chin. "My dear," Mistress said, her voice kind, "it's perfectly acceptable to be proud of your work here. I will not punish you, nor will I allow anyone else to do so."

Abigail swallowed down the unexpected lump in her throat. "Yes, Mistress."

The corners of Mistress's lips twitched and Abigail realized she was staring at the woman's mouth. Quickly, she turned back to the new gown for Turquoise Sky. "How is she doing?"

Mistress sighed heavily. "Nonoci is healing. She will take much work before she can be Miss Sky. That poor girl has been used so hard..." She seemed lost in thought. "I think I shall have to do something about *that*."

Abigail shivered at the icy edge to Mistress's voice. She had been used plenty hard herself. To imagine something worse than Mr. Dawson...

She took a deep breath and pushed that dark year away. Besides, that was the past. This was her future. This dress—all of the dresses—were her freedom.

"It will be all right, dear," Mistress said, smoothing out her skirts. "I will take care of her, just as I took care of you. Of all of you." Mistress stepped in and touched her palm to Abigail's cheek.

"Thank you, Mistress," Abigail repeated.

Mistress regarded her for a long moment. Years of looking placid kicked in and Abigail schooled her features into a blank nothingness. "Ebony, may I ask you a question?"

"Of course, Mistress." She didn't see why Mistress had to ask if she could ask a question.

"I've spoken with Opal. She remarked how much you enjoy...*performing*, shall we say, with her for the gratification of certain gentlemen callers."

Abigail ducked her head, although she knew it was pointless to try and hide the blush from Mistress. "I just wanted to make sure that Mr. Kerr is pleased with us."

Which was true, because she enjoyed the money she got when there were three people in bed just as much a she enjoyed the money she got when there were two people in bed. Abigail and Opal had fallen into an arrangement of sorts and had taken on the bulk of these requests, especially from Mr. Kerr, the undertaker. Sometimes the men joined in, but sometimes—like Mr. Kerr—they didn't, leaving Abigail and Opal to their own amusements.

Abigail had come to look forward to these nights. Opal was soft and smooth and gentle. Her touch excited Abigail as no man's had. There was tenderness there and Abigail had long since realized that she did not have to act with Opal.

All of these thoughts raced through Abigail's head. And she was sure that, if she looked up and met Mistress's gaze, the older woman would see all written on her face.

"Opal thinks that you have quite a way with a woman."

Abigail didn't reply because she had no idea what to say. "I'm happy to serve the men."

Mistress *tsked* immediately. "Ebony, you know better. Please use the correct words. Language is important."

She winced. "I'm happy to continue entertaining our gentlemen callers," she rephrased.

"I have every confidence in you. However, every so often—although rarely—we have a request from a lady who would like to *explore*, shall we say, without the benefit of her husband being in the room." Abigail's cheeks only got hotter. Mistress went on, "Would you be willing to entertain ladies privately? I think you, of all my girls, would best be able to satisfy these special requests."

"What about Opal?" Because Abigail had only been here for two years and Opal had been here for close to four. As best as Abigail understood the situation, Opal should have the first right of refusal.

Mistress waved this away. "Of course Opal will be happy to see to the needs of our customers. And I know she is more than capable—you enjoy her, do you not?"

Abigail squeezed her eyes shut tight, but she nodded all the same.

"But what Opal enjoys more is performing for an audience and I do not believe that, without a gentleman to watch her, she would enjoy taking her time with another woman." Mistress stepped in closer. "Not like you would."

Abigail's heart felt like it was going to beat right out of her chest. She put a hand over it, just to keep it in.

Mistress laughed, a light, sweet sound. She cupped Abigail's cheek in her hand and lifted her face. "My dear girl, do not be embarrassed. Women are soft and wonderful creatures. Besides," she went on in a more businesslike tone. "I will be happy to give you an additional three dollars for these special requests."

Abigail's eyes widened. Three dollars was a lot of money. Every little bit she could add into her savings would get her that much closer to her shop.

But then she remembered herself. "That's all right. I'll be happy to do it for the regular rate."

The lines around Mistress's mouth tightened and her nostrils flared with displeasure. Abigail braced for a blow. But it didn't come. Mistress had never struck her. As far as Abigail knew, Mistress never struck any of the girls.

Instead, Mistress merely looked disappointed. "Ebony, you are neither enslaved nor my servant. I would hope that, in our time together, I have never treated you as either one."

Abigail quickly shook her head. "Of course not, Mistress."

Mistress sighed heavily and looked up to the ceiling, as if she were praying to the heavens above. "Ebony, you are a businesswoman. I *beg* you remember that. Every single thing I teach you here is a lesson that you will use when you open up your own shop. One day, you will be your own supervisor and you had best learn to act like one now. If you always act the servant, people will always treat you as one and I did not save you so that you could imprison your mind yourself."

Abigail's breath caught in her throat, her eyes

burning. Mistress was right, as always. Here at the Jeweled Ladies, she was afforded more respect and power than she'd ever had. The other girls and Mistress didn't treat her as a servant or even a companion. Abigail was the one who ducked her head and jumped to do extra chores.

But it was hard to hope for something better. Before she'd come here, hope had never gotten her far in life.

Mistress put her arm around Abigail's shoulders and gave her a quick hug. "You have come far, my dear. But we have a ways to go before you're ready to open your shop. So when I offer you three dollars, a businesswoman would say *make it five*. You are a free woman and, as such, you need to learn to stick up for yourself. Now," she went on, clasping her hands in front of her. "Let's try that again. I will offer you an additional three dollars for every curious lady who requests your services."

Abigail swallowed. Everything Mistress had said was true. She was a free woman now, finally free. They were almost equals, in a fashion. But the lessons she had learned at Mrs. Whithall's and Mr. Dawson's hands were hard to break.

Still, Mistress had invested in her, making her more than she could have been on her own. Mistress had taught her polish and given her room to make her dresses. Mistress believed, with all of her heart, that one day Abigail would get that shop, and so very few people had ever believed in Abigail.

She could not let Mistress down. "I would be delighted to entertain ladies for an additional five dollars," she said, unable to stop the waver in her voice.

Money and manners would go a long way toward her dream—but none of that changed one simple fact. She couldn't read and, thus far, Mistress had made no effort to teach her. Nor had anyone else. A whispering, nagging fear in the back of her mind said that Mistress only told her that she wanted her to open up a shop because it was what Abigail dearly wanted to hear—but Mistress had no plans of letting her go. She was too valuable on her back and her dresses were too fine.

That was what Mr. Dawson had said, too. Abigail was too good, too important to leave the shop, to talk to anyone but customers, to do anything but sew, sew, *sew.* Slowly, the man she'd apprenticed herself to had narrowed her world to a tiny room. And she'd let it happen until she was trapped and completely at his mercy.

Mistress had offered to find her a position working in a kitchen or as a maid. But Abigail wanted her own dress shop. She didn't want to rely on someone else making decisions for her. She didn't want to be at anyone else's mercy.

Mistress had told her that, as a maid, she might earn sixty dollars a year. As a whore, she might earn that in a night.

Mr. Dawson had ruined Abigail. Why cling to her virtue when doing so would keep her scrubbing floors for years and years to come? If she saved her earnings, she could have her shop in another two years. Maybe less. She already had twenty-three hundred dollars saved. Another thousand, maybe, and she'd never be beholden to anyone.

"Wonderful," Mistress said, looking more pleased than Abigail would have given her credit for, considering she had just voluntarily agreed to give up more money. "Now," she went on. What else was there to discuss? "I have a surprise for you."

"Oh?"

"Do you recall the rather drab woman I was speaking to in the dry-goods store the other day? While you were choosing fabrics for Miss Sky?"

Abigail nodded. It was uncommon for Mistress to talk with one of the prim town ladies for as long as she had. And *drab* was, unfortunately, the right word for that lady. Her sad bonnet and ill-fitting dress did nothing to flatter her figure.

One of Abigail's gifts was that she could look at a woman—any woman—and see the potential. That was why she had been valuable to Mr. Dawson and why she was valuable to Mistress—her dresses played up the assets of the Jewels to their finest.

And although that woman had been scowling and swaddled in far too much brown wool, Abbey could see where there was beauty in her. Her face was strong and proud and the lines of her shoulders suggested a graceful body under those ungraceful clothes. "Of course, Mistress. Why do you ask?"

Wait—had they had been discussing the drab lady the entire time? Perhaps that scowling face had made an illicit request—for a girl. For Abigail.

That drab woman was not Opal. Opal was soft and giggly and teasing. But the thought of touching that other woman...a thrill of anticipation shivered down Abigail's back. What would that woman look like without that sack of a dress or that lifeless bonnet? What would she look like, laid out on a soft bed with her spectacles cast aside and her hair unbound?

Beautiful, Abigail guessed.

"*That* was Miss Minerva Krenshaw," Mistress explained. "She is the schoolteacher in Brimstone. And I believe that she is willing to tutor you in your letters."

Abigail gasped, clutching her hands to her chest. She might learn how to read! "Oh," she gasped. "Would she?"

"There are conditions," Mistress said, her voice reining in Abigail's excitement. "She cannot be seen in the Jeweled Ladies and she will not allow you in the schoolhouse. She values her reputation within this community above all else and she will not accept any money that we have earned in our way."

Abigail frowned. "I don't understand."

"I believe I have the solution," Mistress went on. "Rev. Mays—you remember him, dear, don't you? Oh, I suppose he normally sees Garnet. Anyway, he has agreed to allow you and Miss Krenshaw to meet in the Methodist Church. And as for payment to the schoolmarm..." She shrugged, a delicate shoulder lifting and falling with infinite grace. "Perhaps you could sew her a dress."

Chapter Three

This was wrong. Minerva wasn't even a Methodist and she had heard whispers that the Rev. Mays was just as much a sinner as anyone else in this town. That was the sort of detail that few saw fit to share with her, but she wasn't stupid. She heard the whispers behind gloved hands and fans when the Reverend walked by.

Minerva was a good Baptist. Well, maybe not as good of a Baptist as she liked to think she was. After all, she was now sneaking into the Methodist Church through a side door in order to teach a soiled dove to read.

Surely, the good that she was hoping to accomplish here outweighed the immorality of this entire situation. This was a Christian duty of hers—to teach this woman to read so that she could escape the bonds of prostitution. Wasn't that why Minerva taught? It was a higher calling, to help her fellow man—and woman—better themselves.

If only all of this bettering didn't have to come with a compromise of her morals. If only she could have the money for books and supplies for her school without having to take it from a former prostitute—the mayor's wife. If only she could help the young colored woman without having to clandestinely meet in a Methodist Church, of all places.

If only Miss White hadn't caught Minerva looking in the dry-goods store.

The Methodist Church was grander than her Baptist Church. Workers were extending the steeple to accommodate a new bell being shipped in all the way from the foundries of Philadelphia and stunning stained glass had been installed in three of the windows. The Baptist Church was little more than a shack with pews. It was hot in summer and cold in the winter, but none of that mattered because that was where Minerva felt most holy. The Methodist Church was too great by half. That money could have been better spent on Bibles or the school, or even a library.

No one noticed her as she slipped around the back and opened the small door at the side of the vestibule. But then, no one ever noticed her. Being unremarkable afforded her a certain measure of freedom and Minerva was sorry to say that she took advantage of that whenever she could.

The Methodist Church was large enough to have a second story with additional seats in the balcony. That was where Minerva headed now. If anyone came looking for her or Miss White, it would be easy to stay hidden.

She took the stairs carefully, testing each one for creaks. Once she had reached the balcony, Minerva peered into the darkness. There—a small window set into the building and a pew right underneath it. That would provide enough light for her and Miss White to read the books together.

Together. The word sent a sinful shiver down her back as she recalled the way the young woman's face brightened when Minerva had caught her eye.

21

She made her way over to the shaft of sunlight and settled in to wait. School had let out for the day at three. She was supposed to meet Miss White at four and the lesson would go until five. Normally during those hours, Minerva saw to her chores. She cooked her meals on the stove in the corner of the schoolroom next to her desk. She did her washing. She prepared her lessons for the next day. If she had a free moment, she read old newspapers—the only ones she could afford were the ones discarded from the Golden Star hotel.

And she did so alone. Her students raced off and their parents were still working. No one would miss her for an hour a few times a week. She hoped. Oh, how she hoped.

She stared out that little window, watching the town move below her. This was how it always was—Minerva separate from those around her. But it was better that way. If she got too friendly with the townspeople, they might start asking questions—questions Minerva did not want to answer. Did she want to get married? Would she like to meet their friend or their cousin, someone who was looking for a good wife who was good with children?

To those people on the streets below her, that was the natural order of things. A schoolmarm would either be married off or live her life as a hopeless old spinster. And spinsterhood was by far the more preferable of the two options.

She saw Miss White coming half a block away. Black was the color of mourning and few women looked good in it. The fabric of her dress had a rich sheen to it—and probably cost as much as Minerva made in a year. The skirt bustled high on Miss White's backside, but there was a scandalous slit in the fabric that flashed her calf with every step. She had a matching black parasol that appeared to be nothing but expensive lace—fringe hanging on the tips, swaying with her every step.

No, no, *no*. Minerva was stronger than temptation and that was that.

Miss White disappeared from view. Would that scandalous woman walk through the front door as if she belonged in a church? Or would she slip through the side as Minerva had done?

The front door creaked. Of course.

Miss White walked down the center aisle until she was in the very middle of the church and then she paused. Her eyes searched the cavernous building—the altar, the windows, the rows of pews then, to Minerva's surprise, Miss White strode forward to the altar and fell to her knees before the holy cross. She dropped her head in prayer and held her pose for a long moment.

Minerva stepped back. She felt like she was intruding on a private moment. Far be it from her to get between a woman and her God. Even if that woman was a soiled dove.

But she didn't look away. Miss White wore her hair piled high on her head, and under a hat that matched the dress perfectly. At this angle, Minerva could see the graceful slope of her neck and smooth expanse of her shoulders.

She really was a beautiful creature. But as Minerva stared at her, she thought she saw a flaw on Miss White's skin that dipped below the edge of the dress. An imperfection? Or a scar, perhaps?

Before she could decide, Miss White rose to her feet and turned. Across the vestibule, their eyes met and Minerva had the sensation of prickling along her skin. With a faint smile, Miss White picked up her parasol. Minerva retreated to her seat underneath the shaft of sunlight and waited, her heart beating wildly.

She wasn't nervous. She had been a schoolteacher for ten years now—ever since she had turned eighteen. There had been a period of time during which, when she had had a particularly unruly group of older boys with a penchant for cruelty, she had even carried a gun. She had faced down belligerent parents and angry councilmen, all without batting an eye.

But none of that mattered as Miss White ascended the stairs and the balcony. All of Minerva's flinty bravery dissolved under the full force of Miss White's smile.

Lead me not into temptation, Minerva silently prayed. Because that's what Miss White was— temptation come to life and writ large.

The dress had been beautiful at a distance but up close, Minerva could see lace flounces and glimmering beadwork all over the bodice. It was black, but it caught the eye, practically commanding that Minerva stare. At this woman's bosom.

Luckily, instincts took over and saved her from mortal embarrassment. She checked the watch she wore pinned high on her chest. "You are early." It was three forty-eight.

Miss White paused, her smile tightening. "I thought it best not to keep you waiting," she said, her voice lilting gently with a thick southern accent. "Thank you for agreeing to this."

24

Minerva gritted her teeth. She would not let that accent or that dress be her undoing. She was a stronger woman this, by God. "I have but one request," she said, mentally wincing at how grating her northern accent sounded in comparison to Miss White's.

"Oh?" Miss White came to sit on the pew with a scant two feet between her and Minerva. Close enough to touch. "And what is that? Is it..."

She reached out, hesitated, and then plucked the bonnet strings underneath Minerva's chin. Miss White didn't touch her, but Minerva felt a bolt of electricity run through her body all the same. She watched helplessly as Miss White pulled the bonnet—shapeless and threadbare, just like everything else she owned—from her head and set it aside.

"Is it something *personal*?"

Minerva forced her lungs to work. Unfortunately, that breath was scented with Miss White's perfume—lavender. Lavender with something sweet underneath, like vanilla, perhaps. "Absolutely not," she snapped, taking refuge in her temperament. "I have no need for any of your services." And then, to her horror, she heard herself add, "and even if I did, I would not partake of you."

The young woman unpinned her hat. "I would like to pay you for your time. And if you will not accept my money, then I am handy with a needle. And I must say," she added, casting a surprisingly critical eye over Minerva's clothes, "that you could do with a new dress. More than likely, you could do with a new everything."

Indignation flared. "I beg your pardon, young lady. I have no need for fancy silks and velvets. I am dressed appropriately for my station."

25

For a moment, Miss White seemed almost...cowed. Her shoulders rolled forward and she seemed almost to curl into herself. Instantly, Minerva regretted her abrasiveness. But she also didn't because she needed Miss White to stay well clear of her.

Miss White rallied and Minerva couldn't help but admire her for it. "That may be, but the fabric is too heavy for this part of Texas, and besides, it's worn bare. You would look better in a navy than that brown and your shawl, I'm sorry to say, isn't even fit to be used as a rag. I promise you that I am fully capable of making a dress that retains the modesty you prize while fitting you better and making your life easier." Miss White turned her head to the side and studied Minerva's dress. "I could make you a light summer dress out of muslin and a serviceable winter dress out of wool. You will be more comfortable."

This was, if possible, even more unsettling than it had been when Mistress had apprised her person. They were in a church, for God's sake. "Comfort is overrated," she snapped. "And there's nothing wrong with my clothes. Brown is a perfectly fine color."

Miss White worried her lower lip with teeth that were surprisingly even. "You must allow me to repay you for your kindness. I will not be your charity case."

Now it was Minerva's turn to look away. It wasn't so much the dresses. It would be the act of Miss White taking Minerva's measurements, fitting the pieces to her while she stood wearing nothing but her underthings. A custom-made dress would, by necessity, strip her nearly bare and leave her vulnerable and exposed to far more than just a misplaced needle.

"I'm a skilled seamstress," Miss White went on, the new edge to her voice. "I have been sewing dresses for ladies of quality since I was eight. And if you choose to believe wearing the dress you are wearing is a reflection of what you consider your fine qualities, I beg to tell you that you are sorely mistaken. The dress is too large, it is worn smooth in too many places to count. Your gloves are shabby and your bonnet is the saddest thing I've ever seen that dared call itself a hat. I can tell just by looking at you that your stays fit you all wrong. I would dare say that your underthings are just as pitiful as the dress. I do not think the Lord requires us to forgo pride in our appearance. How can you expect the community to respect your when you do not take pains to respect yourself?" Her eyes flashed. "Unless you want to be seen as a pitiful, helpless thing who cannot even dress herself."

Minerva gaped at her. "You have a quick tongue, for a girl who cannot read."

Miss White looked as if Minerva had slapped her face and indeed, it felt as if Minerva had. "I cannot read because slaves are not taught to read. It does not mean I am stupid."

"I did not realize." Humiliation burned her cheeks. Her parents would be horrified by her behavior right now. Hadn't she been raised to believe that all men—and women—were created equal? "I apologize," Minerva said, surprised to hear her voice shaking. "That was uncalled for and I shall not speak to you like that again." Miss White did not return her gaze and Minerva felt as if she needed to say something more.

But what? She knew she was a shrew but she had

always prided herself on being fair. And yet there was something about this young woman that turned her about and left her dizzy from the spinning. "I..."

Miss White stood, smoothed the skirt of her elaborate dress. "There is no need to explain. I'm just a colored girl—and a whore at that," she said with only a trace of bitterness in her voice. Instead, she mostly just sounded resigned. And sad. It was the sadness that cut Minerva the deepest. "I am still learning how to negotiate as a businesswoman. I see I have much farther to go. I am sorry that I overstepped my bounds."

Miss White picked up her hat and gave Minerva a blank-looking smile. Minerva didn't like that smile. It was the look of surrender. "I thank you for taking the time to meet with me," Miss White said in an equally blank voice. "Many in your position would not have even agreed to this." Effortlessly, she fixed the hat back on her pile of hair, tucked her parasol under her arm, and made for the stairs that would lead her away from this balcony and away from Minerva. She paused and looked back over her shoulder, her face hidden in shadows. "I am sorry I offended you. You must know that I think you are a lovely woman, despite the clothes, and it was wrong of me to speak out of place."

A lovely woman. It should have been a taunt because Minerva was anything but that. However, the sincerity in Miss White's voice—Minerva didn't think that was faked.

Suddenly it seemed too important that she and Miss White not part on these terms. "Wait." Miss White froze, but she did not turn back to Minerva. "Your Mistress—she said you were going to open a shop."

Slowly, Miss White turned around. She was still deep in the shadows of the balcony. "That is my hope. To have my own shop… That would truly be freedom."

"And you need me for that?" Minerva winced. That hadn't come out right.

"I need to read to keep the ledger, to take orders." Miss White paused, and then took a step back toward where Minerva stood. "But I need to sew a dress for you, too. Right now, the only people who will let me sew for them are the other girls at the Jeweled Ladies—and Mrs. Dupree. But if I could have a woman such as yourself," she said, her voice changing into something more pleading, "someone who is deeply respected in the community and known for her righteousness—wear one of my dresses, people will see I can do so much more than just sluttish gowns and corsets. That would go a long way toward helping me change my station."

Miss White must have known that statement was the one thing that could change Minerva's mind. This woman was nothing but a temptation—but could Minerva really turn her back on the young woman and consign all of her hopes and dreams to the rubbish pile?

"You must promise me," Minerva told her, trying to sound as stern as she could, "that you will use this knowledge to escape that cursed brothel."

"I swear it."

"Then…" Minerva swallowed down her nerves and all her misgivings. "Then we shall proceed."

"You mean it?" Miss White clapped her hands.

"Of course. I give you my word." That was it, then. She was committed to this endeavor, however much a folly or a sin it would be.

"Oh!" Unexpectedly, Miss White rushed up to

her and grasped Minerva's hands in hers. "I'm...oh, I'm so excited! Oh, thank you, Miss Krenshaw. I—again, I'm sorry for stepping out of line." Her words spilled out of her so fast that all Minerva could do was stand there and let Miss White hold her hands. "I'm trying to remember how to negotiate and stand up for myself and it's still a tricky balance. You have no idea what this means to me!"

"Please, stop apologizing. I am the one who is being difficult," Minerva said, jerking her hands away before something completely forbidden happened, like the young woman sweeping her into an enthusiastic hug. At the thought, that odd prickling skittered over Minerva's skin again and, ugly as it was, she was thankful for the dress that covered everything. "It is my chief character defect, although a useful one in the schoolroom." She took a deep breath. Nervously, she glanced over the balcony edge, but she didn't see anyone else in the church. "We shall have some rules."

Miss White nodded, trying to look contrite and failing miserably. "Of course."

"Lessons first. Dresses second." Miss White nodded again, so Minerva went on. "Do you have anything less scandalous to wear?"

The color at Miss White's cheeks deepened. "Of course. I have the dress I wear to church."

"Oh? And which church do you attend?"

"I'm Catholic, Miss."

Minerva sighed heavily. As if this couldn't get worse. A Baptist spinster and a Catholic soiled dove in clandestine meetings in a Methodist Church. She pinched the bridge of her nose. How had she come to this place in her life? "We might as well get started."

30

Chapter Four

Abigail sat on her bed, staring down at the piece of paper in her hand. There were four words written on that page, two full names.

Ebony White and Abigail Whithall.

She didn't recognize the words. But Miss Minerva Krenshaw had carefully written them across the page. "These are your names," the prickly woman had said. "No one can take them away from you."

Abigail's eyes grew wet just staring at the words. With the tip of a knitting needle, she lightly traced over the letters, careful not to poke a hole in the paper. Miss Krenshaw had said to do that—holding a knitting needle would be like holding a pencil. Abigail was supposed to say the names of the letters out loud as she traced over them.

Not for the first time, she wished Mrs. Whithall had taught her to read. Mrs. Whithall had been a kind-enough woman. Her daughter, Miss Catherine, had been Abigail's closest friend. They were like sisters, except Abigail had been enslaved. Mrs. Whithall had treated Abigail decently, even giving her the Whithall name. As Miss Catherine's companion, Abigail had gotten to go to church weekly. She had gotten to sit in on lessons for the piano and French. That never stopped amusing her—she was fluent in French but couldn't read either language.

Mrs. Whithall had indulged Miss Catherine. When Miss Catherine had learned to sew, Abigail had learned to sew. And when Abigail had dared to surpass Miss Catherine with her skills, Mrs. Whithall had not beaten her. Instead, she had provided Abigail with more supplies. There had been long, glorious afternoons of cutting patterns and staring at fashion plates and sewing new dresses for dolls and then, later, for Miss Catherine and Mrs. Whithall herself. On special occasions—her birthday, Christmas—Abigail had even been allowed to sew a dress for herself.

Abigail had had a kind of security that most enslaved people didn't have. She'd had a nice house and plenty of good food and something close to a friendship born of love with Miss Catherine. It had not been a bad life. Abigail knew that Mrs. Whithall was not the worst of people and Miss Catherine...Abigail missed her still.

Being Mrs. Whithall's slave had been a life of menial drudgery. But being Miss Catherine's constant companion had been moments of sweetness in an otherwise hard life. As Abigail's sewing had gotten better, Miss Catherine had been the one to say, "You should have your own shop, Abigail. Even white women would buy dresses from you. Mother would." That offhand statement had become Abigail's entire reason to hope.

Abigail did not regret Mrs. Whithall's death of a fever that had swept through Lexington, but she sorely wished that same fever hadn't carried off Miss Catherine.

If only Mrs. Whithall had taught Abigail to read. But she had never been the Whithall's family. Just Mrs. Whithall's property, the only slave the widowed woman could afford. Abigail had had to get up at the crack of dawn to light the fires and clean their small house in Lexington. As soon as she'd been able, she'd taken on the cooking duties as well, to save money on a second servant.

She'd been responsible for helping both Whithall women fix their hair and dress. Mrs. Whithall was particular about how she liked her hair done and, especially when she'd been a little girl, the white woman would slap Abigail if she didn't get it right. Once, Mrs. Whithall had even hit her with the hot tongs, leaving a burn on Abigail's arm. She still had the scar.

Miss Catherine would have taught Abigail to read, but she was afraid of what her mother would do if she had been caught. So Abigail had toiled in her ignorance.

That very ignorance had led her to put her faith in Mr. Dawson when he'd said he'd help her become a proper seamstress. If she knew how to read, she'd never again be at anyone's mercy. She would be her own woman.

"These are your names," Miss Krenshaw had said. "No one can take them away from you."

She smiled. It had taken years, but Mrs. Whithall couldn't stop Abigail now. She was going to read. She was going to open a shop. She was going to be her own woman.

And she was never going to be a slave. Not again. Not ever.

Still, reading was not a singular gift that could be opened, like a present in a box. All good things were worth the hard work. So she studied the names. She knew the *A*. So that word and the word after that were her name—her true name. Abigail Whithall. That was who she was. Ebony White was just a role she played.

There was a soft knock on the door. "Yes?"

Mistress popped her head into the door. "How did it go with the schoolteacher?"

Abigail thought back to the way Miss Krenshaw's eyes had widened when Abigail had plucked the sad bonnet off her head. The way she'd gasped when Abigail had criticized her equally sad dress. She'd been insulted, yes. But Abigail had seen the way her pulse fluttered in her neck, the way her eyes had darkened, the way her chest had heaved.

There was something there that went beyond the normal moral censure people of Miss Krenshaw's station normally directed at women like Abigail.

Abigail had learned much during her time at the Jeweled Ladies and unless she was mistaken, Miss Krenshaw—with her prickly defensiveness and wide brown eyes—had been gripped by something that looked like attraction.

"I do not think she likes me," she said to Mistress. At the very least, Miss Krenshaw did not *want* to like her.

Mistress stepped fully into the room and shut the door behind her, looking like a schoolgirl about to indulge in some gossip. "*Really,*" was all she said. It was not a question.

Abigail didn't allow the smile to dance across her lips. Mistress was the keenest judge of character

Abigail had ever known. Had she seen something in Miss Krenshaw? The same *something* that Abigail had seen?

"I think she will let me sew her a dress—no doubt, she needs everything to go with it. I've never seen a sadder sack of fabric on a woman in my entire life."

Mistress had such a beautiful smile. Going with this strange woman who offered her protection—it could have been a trap, just like the one Mr. Dawson had laid for her.

But it was that smile that had made Abigail's decision for her. Mistress had smiled at her and promised that she would keep Abigail safe from Mr. Dawson and that she would have her own shop. Mistress had promised Abigail that she would be free.

"Did you make all of the arrangements, then?"

Abigail nodded. "We are to meet every Monday, Wednesday, and Thursday, from four until five at the Methodist Church. She will provide me with a slate and books, although I told her I would be happy to pay for my own. But she said that I was a student and all students got the same courtesy."

Mistress noticed the paper in Abigail's lap. "What did she give you?"

"My name. My names," Abigail quickly corrected. For a moment, she hesitated to show her names to Mistress. But Mistress would not destroy it out of spite. Abigail was sure of it.

So she held up the paper. Mistress handled it gently, as if she realized how special it was, too. "Miss Krenshaw has a lovely hand," she said, handing the paper back. "There may even be a lovely woman underneath all of that shapeless cloth. I do hope she lets you sew her a dress. Or three," she added with a grin. "I have a feeling that you can do amazing things with her."

"You don't mind if I spend that much time with her?" Four o'clock was the unofficial beginning of the evening at the Jeweled Ladies. Although most of the customers wouldn't begin to filter in until after the supper hour, it was expected that there would be one or two girls available earlier in the evening. Older gentlemen, widowers especially, did not keep late hours.

Mistress waved this suggestion away. "Your time is your own, Ebony. You may do with it as you wish— you know that. And I believe this will be time well spent."

Abigail exhaled a breath she hadn't realized she'd been holding. Mr. Dawson would have said no, better to focus on the task at hand. She absolutely wouldn't have been able to take time out of the workday to do something as unnecessary as learning to read. And if Abigail had protested...

She shuddered.

Mistress went on, "But do try to have a care for Miss Krenshaw."

As if Miss Krenshaw could not defend herself. The woman was all spiky, like a porcupine. Before she could think better of it, Abigail rolled her eyes. And then she tensed, because that was the sort of gesture that had gotten her slapped back before. But of course, no such blow came. "She does *not* like me," Abigail repeated.

"On the contrary," Mistress said, opening the

door. "She does not like Ebony White. And," she said, nodding toward the piece of paper that had once again taken a position in Abigail's lap, "it is quite clear that isn't who you are, is it?"

Then she was gone, shutting Abigail's door softly.

Abigail traced her name again and again, pondering the meaning of both. She had put Abigail Whithall aside to embrace Ebony White.

Ebony White was in charge of her own fate, learning to navigate being free, becoming a businesswoman. Abigail Whithall had not been able to do any of those things.

Abigail wasn't Ebony White but she didn't think she was the same Abigail Whithall either. Not anymore. She was someone new. Smarter. Stronger. More willing to fight for herself. This new woman knew what she wanted and would do what it took to get it.

She wondered if this new Abigail was someone whom Miss Krenshaw might, in fact, like.

*

Today, Minerva had tried. She had put on her Sunday dress, her very best one. She had taken extra time braiding her hair back so that it lay smooth against her scalp. She had polished her glasses and watch. Heavens, she had even tried to affix a bit of lace to the edge of her bonnet, the only lace she had kept from New York.

And for what? Why had she indulged in this little bit of vanity?

37

"Good afternoon, Miss Krenshaw."

For her. Vanity was a sin but so was lying and besides, God would be able to see into her heart and know the truth.

Minerva had taken care with dressing today for her—Miss White. Or…Miss Whithall?

"We did not determine last time what I should call you," she began, already feeling the prickliness rise up in her.

Because it seemed to Minerva that thinking of this girl as Ebony White or even Miss White only made the situation worse. That was the name of a Jewel. That was the name of someone whom Minerva could not help—or, at the very least, should not.

But this lovely young woman—today, wearing another black dress that covered most of her arms and a great deal more of her chest, even if the fabric did cling to her every curve—last time, she had told Minerva her real name. Abigail Whithall. And that woman was someone else entirely.

Instead of silk or velvet, the dress was a dull bombazine, not a fabric that invited fingers to stroke or the eye to linger. It was perilously close to decent. Funereal, but decent.

"What would you like to call me?"

Minerva shook her head. "None of that. You are woman of means. You must present yourself as you wish the world to see you."

A smile flickered across her lips and Minerva felt her gaze drawn. She had never worn makeup. Such adornment was sinful. But this woman had lips that had been painted a deep ruby red—temptingly red, like the apple from which Eve had taken a bite.

38

Not Miss White, Minerva silently prayed.

"If I am to call you Miss Krenshaw, then you should call me Miss Whithall, should you not?"

Minerva exhaled breath she hadn't realized she had been holding. "Just so," she managed to say crisply.

"But," Miss Whithall went on, touching a single manicured finger to her cheek, "If I were to call you Minerva—because we are equals—would you call me Abigail?"

It was the first time this girl had said Minerva's name. She was Miss Krenshaw. It was her entire identity. Miss Krenshaw was proper and moral. She was stern and strict, but fair. She was…

Miss Krenshaw was poorly dressed, prickly. She was invisible.

Her own words came back to her. *You must present yourself as you wish the world to see you.*

How did she want this woman to see her?

Slowly, she drew in another breath, straightening her back until she could've piled ten books atop her head. "We are equals," she said carefully. "But I would thank you not to call me Minerva outside of our tutoring sessions. *Abigail*," she added deliberately.

She wanted to say the name again and again. She wanted to move her tongue over it as if it was a peppermint stick, slowly savoring every little bit of sweetness.

This time, the smile did not flicker. It took up residence upon her deep red lips and spread warmth through her entire face. "No one else calls me Abigail, either. It shall be just between us."

Oh, this felt dangerous. Secrets with the soiled

dove? Most dangerous, indeed. It was a great effort, but Minerva managed to tear her gaze away from Abigail. There, on the pew, was a wicker basket. "What did you bring?"

"My sewing supplies. I thought that after we worked on my letters, I could take your measurements." Again her head tilted to the side as her gaze sharpened. It made Minerva want to cross her arms in front of her chest and try to hide. "Although I think I have a good understanding of your shape already. But it is hard to tell in those clothes."

As she had for several nights now, Minerva tried to figure out a way to allow Abigail to repay her for her services as a tutor. And, as she had for several nights now, she failed to come up with anything else that this young, beautiful woman had that Minerva wanted.

Her cheeks heated. There was nothing else, she told herself. Nothing at all. "Then let us get to our letters. Did you practice tracing your names?"

"With a knitting needle, like you said." Abigail settled back on to the pew, leaving just enough room for Minerva to take up position at the other end. Blissfully, the wicker basket sat between them.

Never before had Minerva been so grateful to an inanimate object as she was to that basket. She produced the slate and chalk that she had brought from the schoolroom and set it on top of the basket. "Good," she said as she wrote Abigail Whithall across the slate. Then she handed the chalk over and turned the slate so that it faced her pupil. "Let's begin, shall we?"

For the next hour, they worked diligently. Abigail's hand was steady with the chalk in it. They wrote her name over and over again, pronouncing each letter and identifying every sound

As the five o'clock hour approached, Minerva was pleased to note that Abigail's signature had begun to take shape. "Your signature is your calling card in the world," she reminded Abigail. "You will sign your name to letters and bills and invoices. It is the mark you will leave upon the world."

She looked up at her student—only to realize that Abigail was far less than a foot away from. Their foreheads were so close together as to be almost touching. They had been bent over the slate—but that was not where Minerva's attention was suddenly focused.

Lavender and vanilla surrounded her. There was another note underneath that, a sweet oil perhaps. Did Abigail use it to dress her hair? Or was that part of the red lips—lips that were now only inches away from hers?

Minerva absolutely needed to move. To move *away*, she quickly corrected. She needed to stand and put some distance between her and her student.

"I couldn't help but notice," Abigail said as she tugged the strings of Minerva's bonnet loose, "that you added some lace."

Minerva could feel her sweet breath bouncing off her skin. She needed to put space between them. But she couldn't. "It made sense, what you said last time. To dress respectably is to be thought respectable."

Move, she ordered herself. *Move.* And it did seem like movement happened. But she would swear that she got closer to Abigail—not further away.

Oh, it wasn't fair, how pretty she was when her lips curved like that. Minerva realized that she was physically shaking from the effort of keeping her hands to herself.

"Shall I take your measurements now, Minerva?" Abigail whispered softly.

Minerva barely heard her for the pounding in her ears. "Promise you will make me respectable? I mean," she quickly corrected, "make me *look* respectable?" Because she was already respectable. Respectable and honorable and…and…

All thoughts left her mind as Abigail reached over and plucked the top button of her dress, the one right under her chin. "Would it be all right," she asked in that same soft voice that had Minerva leaning forward to catch her words, "if I asked you to step out of this dress?"

"Why?" Panic rose up in the back of her throat like the taste of blood.

"This is how you get a dress made for you." Then, mercifully, Abigail stood. "If I don't take your measurements, it won't fit properly."

Minerva knew that. She had gone with her mother to a dress shop in Albany on more than one occasion. She had just been hoping to avoid it *now*.

She opened her mouth to say as much but then made the mistake of looking up at Abigail's face. The young woman stood before her, her hands clasped almost primly in front of her. But that wasn't what stopped Minerva. It was the look on Abigail's face— the same look that Minerva had only caught a glimpse of through the dry-goods store window.

It was almost as if she could see more to Minerva. Honestly, she didn't know if it was a good thing or not.

42

"It will be perfectly proper," Abigail added, worry taking hold around her eyes. "I would prefer not to do this in the church... But besides that, there is nothing improper about this at all."

Lies, all of it. Well, except for that bit about doing it in the church. But what were the alternatives? She could go back to the Jeweled Ladies and strip down for this woman. Or bring her back to the schoolhouse and disrobe for her there. The only other possible option was to take a room at the Golden Star hotel.

All three involved her and Abigail alone in a room with a bed and very little clothing separating them.

As immoral as it was, the church was by far the safest option.

But she had to try just one more time. "Are you sure this is necessary?"

Abigail smiled and then did the worst thing in the world she could have done—she reached down and took Minerva's hands in hers, pulling her to her feet. "But of course," she murmured. "Would you like me to undo the buttons for you?"

"I shall..." she swallowed. Hard. "I shall do them myself

Lead me not into temptation, she prayed as Abigail stepped to the side. Minerva turned her back to attack her buttons, but her fingers were suddenly clumsy and it took her several minutes longer to free herself from the dress. If only she could stop trembling.

"Tell me where you came from," she said, desperate to turn around and see if Abigail was looking at her like a seamstress would or if...

43

No. There was no *if*.

"Lexington, originally. That's where my…" her voice trailed off.

Minerva winced. The people who had owned Abigail. Silently, Minerva gave thanks that slavery was now illegal. "Who were they?"

This was followed by a heavy sigh. "I never knew anything or anyone but the Whithall women. Mrs. Whithall and her daughter, Miss Catherine. Miss Catherine and I were of an age. We grew up almost as sisters."

Almost. What a horrible word. Minerva was able to get another button undone before she asked her next question. "They treated you kindly?"

"As kindly as they might, considering I was their property." There was a mildness to her tone that struck Minerva as deceptive. Why was Abigail trying to make it sound like it was of no import? "They died, though. Mrs. Whithall first. A fever took them both. Miss Catherine gave me my freedom before she passed on."

"That was good of her." Another few buttons gave. "But I am sorry that you were enslaved. It is a cruel, immoral practice."

"It would have been better if she'd defied her mother earlier and taught me to read." Bitterness crept into her voice. Then, after a pause, she added, "Do you really teach colored children at your school?"

The dress began to sag off her shoulders. She probably didn't need to undo any more buttons but she was stalling and she knew it. "Of course. Children need to learn. Informed people are harder to subjugate than those kept in ignorance."

"You were an abolitionist, then?" Was Minerva imagining things or did Abigail sound pleased?

"Yes. Near Albany, upstate New York. My father, God rest his soul, would help runaways cross the border to Canada."

She was still fiddling with the buttons when, unexpectedly, sure hands were on her shoulders, pulling the dress free. "I don't bite," she whispered close to Minerva's ear.

For one of the few times in her life, Minerva wished she were...someone else. Someone bolder, braver. Someone who could not only put a name to what she wanted, but have the wherewithal to take it.

The other times she'd wished to be someone different, she'd wished to be the kind of person who could look at a respectable man of marriageable age and feel something. *Anything.* Anything more than a purely academic interest in their minds or morals.

But now? As Abigail slowly stripped her old dress from her shoulders, Minerva wished that she were the kind of woman who was brave enough to turn to this dove and ask a thoroughly disreputable question. One that went something like, *Would you kiss me?*

Her best dress fell away, leaving her in nothing but her shift and stays and her sad excuse for drawers, as well as her home-knit stockings. Practically *naked.*

"Step out, Minerva." Abigail slid a warm hand under Minerva's arm and helped her balance as she stepped clear of the wool puddled at her feet. Abigail folded the dress and carefully set it to the side, as if it were worth something after all.

"There," Abigail said, her accent warm and inviting. "Let's see what we've got."

Was it a sin to wish that she had pretty underthings? Drawers without holes? Stays that made her bosom look womanly? If it were, Minerva was going to go to hell the moment she died of embarrassment, which, at this rate, would be in the next five seconds.

"Just as I suspected," Abigail said, sounding more like a dressmaker. "That corset is terrible. How can you stand to wear it? It must poke your sides so."

"It serves its purpose." Which was no answer at all. Because the thing did poke her sides and shift dangerously when she sat too quickly. She'd once heard some students whispering that it looked like she had a live ferret under her dress.

Abigail looked at her doubtfully. "And what purpose is that? You'd be just as well served with a hair shirt." Minerva must have grimaced because Abigail's face softened. "My apologies, Minerva. Sometimes we must make do with what we have."

Abigail's gaze drifted back to Minerva's chest and her nipples tightened—without a protective layer of wool to conceal them. *Dear Lord*, she prayed, *please strike me dead now.*

But the Lord did not see fit to end her suffering. Instead, He added to it because Abigail stepped in closer and ran her hand over the front of the corset, making the whole thing shift precariously. "I need this to come off," she murmured, running her fingers underneath the bottom edge. "I can't get a true measurement of you with it on."

"I…" but her words dried up as Abigail somehow got even closer to her and began to slip the busks on her corset free.

Minerva couldn't do a thing except watch as Abigail's dark fingers moved over the aged fabric of her corset. The undergarment put up no resistance and, in seconds, was gone from her waist.

"There we are," Abigail said in a kind voice. Minerva took a deep breath, her waist free of the awful corset. Her bosom seemed to exist in a space that was both a part of her and separate. The cooling air overpowered the thin cotton of her shift and her breasts grew heavy and tight—tighter as Abigail looked her up and down again.

Oh, how Minerva wanted things she couldn't name and didn't dare ask for.

And still the Lord did not see fit to strike her down for her sins.

"Oh, Minerva," Abigail sighed. Then her fingers were running along the neckline of Minerva's shift, plucking at the threadbare fabric. "I am so glad you're letting me do this."

Minerva needed to do something—say something. Anything to get this girl to stop making free with her person and stop saying her name as if she were a precious flower instead of a clod of sunbaked mud.

All she was able to do, however, was close her eyes. Which did block out the image of Abigail's hands moving over her bosom but did nothing to stop Minerva from feeling Abigail's whisper-soft touch.

Her body grew soft and hard at the same time. Longing—painful and real—filled her entire body. "So am I," she heard herself whisper.

So. Apparently one could not die of embarrassment. What else would she learn today?

Chapter Five

Of course this wasn't the proper place to do a dress fitting. Minerva was a God-fearing woman. No wonder she looked so mortified.

Abigail laid the sorriest excuse for a corset that she had ever seen over a dress that was only slightly less awful than the one Minerva had worn last week -and turned her attention back to the woman standing before her. The shift was threadbare and stained. Abigail could see nearly everything through it. Which was not a bad thing. She herself had several shifts made of fine silk that were so sheer nothing could be hidden by them.

Abigail could see Minerva's drawers through that shift—and those were, if possible, in even worse shape. What she could see of the stockings was mildly encouraging. They were knit, more suitable for winter than the warm summer and fall that Brimstone had just had, but they appeared to be in good repair. "Did you make the stockings yourself?" she asked as she stepped back around Minerva to fetch her measuring tape from the basket.

"What? Oh. Yes. I knit. It was a more useful skill in New York. We had winter there, full of cold and snow. Here we just get wind."

Abigail grinned. Minerva was simultaneously both the most practical and the most impractical person Abigail had possibly ever met. Why would anyone wear such things in the peak of Texas heat? "How long have you been in Brimstone?" she asked, as talking about something other than Minerva's clothes seemed to distract the woman.

"Eight years. I left home when I was eighteen and wound up here two years after that."

Abigail ran her gaze over Minerva's body again. Without those horrible clothes, it was as if a whole other woman had been revealed. The schoolteacher, Miss Krenshaw, had a frumpy figure, lumpy in the wrong places. But Minerva?

She was too thin. She didn't have a generous flare at the hips and her bosom, while full, wasn't anything remarkable. But it suited her.

Abigail had an overwhelming urge to pull Minerva's hair free of its artless braid and run her fingers through it. She wanted to see it fall down around Minerva's shoulders.

"Eight years in Brimstone? I've only been here for a little less than two and I'm looking forward to when I can move on."

Minerva took in a shuddering breath. "And you'll open a shop when you leave? Where will you go?"

"San Francisco, maybe. I've heard Virginia City is prospering, too. I'm going to use a measuring tape to take your measurements," Abigail warned. "Just relax."

Minerva snorted. "You're not the one who's practically naked in a church before a woman of…considerable experience." Abigail stepped around her and lifted the measuring tape around her neck. "I'm sorry," Minerva blurted out suddenly. "That was uncalled for."

"It's all right, Minerva." She made a note and then moved the tape measure lower. "We both know what I am and pretending that I am something else would be dishonest. Can you move your arms? I need to take the measurements of your bust."

The color drained out of Minerva's face. "Is that necessary?"

Truthfully, Abigail had no idea what to make of this reaction. Most women who got fitted for a dress understood that this was part of the process. If they were embarrassed about being in nothing but their shift before another woman, they ignored her and the situation. She had taken measurements of so many women wearing next to nothing that she didn't even blink an eye at pulling the tape measure around their back and over their bosoms.

But Minerva was different. "If you tell me what has you worried, I can try to make it better. Is it me? Or just the fact that we're doing this in a church? I'm trying to be gentle, but this won't hurt."

She adjusted the tape measure and pulled it tight. Minerva's shift could not contain the way her nipples had gone tight and there was no hope of disguising the way the hard peaks jutted out toward Abigail.

"It's…" Minerva's voice was little more than the shiver of a leaf in the wind. For all of the world, it sounded like she was whispering sweet nothings into Abigail's ears. "It's *you.*"

Abigail paused, the measuring tape hanging loose around Minerva's waist. "Because I am a woman of ill repute?" For a long moment, Minerva didn't reply. "Or is it because I am a woman?"

Minerva's eyes were still squeezed shut. Her whole body was shaking as she drew in ragged breaths. Color bloomed along her cheeks, an innocent blush.

"I don't know what you're talking about." This should have sounded snappish, Abigail decided. Perhaps it was *supposed* to sound snappish. It was certainly the kind of thing that Miss Krenshaw would say, quick and defensive.

But that wasn't the way it came out. No, to Abigail, it sounded more like a...like a plea. Like an admission that there was a hole in Minerva's education.

Abigail settled her hands on Minerva's waist—tentatively at first, but when Minerva did not jerk away, she spread her fingers wide. "Eight years in Brimstone," Abigail whispered, leaning forward until the stiff tips of Minerva's nipples brushed against the front of her Sunday dress. "And no one has made a wife of you yet?"

If she was wrong—and there was a very real possibility that she was—this would be the point where Minerva snapped. Abigail was indecently close to this spinster schoolteacher. She was implying things that had nothing to do with morality or reputation.

Minerva did not push her away. "No one would have me." Her voice was so soft that Abigail was simply forced to lean in closer, until she could feel Minerva's panting breath against her cheek. "There was no one I wanted."

It all became clear in that moment. The prickly attitude, the terrible dresses. "Maybe you've been asking the wrong kind of people," she said, sliding her hands around Minerva's back. "There's more to this world than just men."

"Oh, God," she said. Then, she tilted her head toward Abigail's. It was a small movement, one that Abigail might have missed if she hadn't been this close.

Abigail didn't miss it.

Of course Abigail had kissed women before. She kissed Opal on a fairly regular basis—kissing and much more than that. But that was for someone else, usually Mr. Kerr. In all honesty, Abigail had never kissed anyone for herself. She had never loved anyone for herself.

And she wanted to. Minerva smelled of soap— lye soap. It was harsh against Abigail's nose but underneath that, there was something else. Lemons, maybe. Something tart.

That was so perfectly Minerva that Abigail smiled. With just a little sugar, lemons were a treat.

Minerva would be a treat. Abigail's treat.

Once, when she had been about thirteen, Miss Catherine had given her an unexpected gift—a pair of silver scissors with engraving on the handle. Abigail had never really had a birthday. She didn't know when she had been born or, for that matter, how old she was. So she had never had birthday gifts. Miss Catherine had saved up her own money and bought Abigail a pair of delicate shears. "Because a dressmaker should have good scissors," the girl had said.

Unwrapping those scissors and knowing they were for her and her alone had sent a bolt of pleasure through Abigail. And *that* was as close as she had ever felt to this feeling right now.

Pleasure. Miss Minerva Krenshaw's lips were warm and delicate under hers and it was indeed pleasurable.

It only got more so when Minerva's hands came up and rested on Abigail's shoulders. For one blissful moment, Minerva sighed into her and Abigail pulled her closer. "*Minerva*."

She shouldn't have spoken because when she did, Minerva pushed her back. "No. No! We can't do this. This is—this is *wrong*."

Abigail stumbled back and sat hard on the pew. "What?"

Minerva began to grab her shabby clothes and throw them on to her body like a woman possessed. "I can't believe I—that you—we can't—oh my God, what have I *done*?"

Oh, no. "Minerva," she tried to say. She needed to apologize and quickly.

But Minerva just shook her head. "This never should have happened. It can't happen." Even though she hadn't gotten buttons lined up on her dress, she grabbed her things and fled for the stairs. Abigail moved to catch her, but Minerva was faster. "It *can't* happen," she repeated and then, just as she started to disappear down the steps, Abigail heard it—the truth of the matter. "*Not again*."

There were advantages to being invisible in a crowd of people. As Minerva hurried home, clutching her shawl in front of her mis-buttoned dress, no one looked at her. No one remarked on her state of disarray. No one noticed her at all.

It took everything she had to make it back to her

schoolhouse before she burst into tears. The shame of it all washed over her.

Even as the mortification tumbled through her head, other thoughts surfaced. Abigail had smelled so sweet. The brush of Minerva's nipples against Abigail's chest—it had been unlike anything she had ever felt before. And when their lips had touched, any moral fortitude that Minerva pretended to possess had nearly blown away on Abigail's sigh.

Oh, she was weak. So very *weak*. A woman was only as good as her reputation and what did Minerva do?

She nearly cast aside her reputation, all because a girl dared to look at her and see something more than a destitute schoolteacher.

Minerva allowed herself to cry for another few minutes but then she did what she always did when life disappointed her—she pulled herself together and got on with living. She changed into one of her regular dresses and brushing out her Sunday best before hanging it back up on the wall in her little room. She checked on the beans she had left simmering on the stovetop.

None of this made her feel any better but idle hands were the Devil's workshop so she finally dug out her knitting and tried to think rationally. She couldn't leave Brimstone. She'd signed the annual contract. To abandon her post now would be unconscionable. No, she was here for another eight months at the very minimum because she kept her promises.

She had agreed to tutor Abigail Whithall. Two lessons did not an education make.

But she could not—*could not*—allow herself to be led into temptation again. It didn't matter that Abigail had kissed her first. All that mattered was that Minerva had been in a compromising position with another person. Another woman.

A woman who had sex with other people for money. While unmarried.

The woman was sin embodied.

But aside from that kiss, Abigail didn't seem a sinner. Not like Mistress was. Instead, Abigail seemed an earnest young lady intent on bettering herself.

But could Minerva see her again, sit close with their heads bent over the slate and not be tempted? Could she honor her promise without dishonoring herself?

She didn't know. But she supposed that she would find out on Wednesday, at four o'clock, when she once again met Abigail in the balcony of the Methodist Church.

Maybe… Yes. She could pretend like nothing had happened and perhaps Abigail would have the decency to do the same. They could go on as they were meant to—the teacher and her student. Nothing more.

But even as she made this resolution, there was still a small, craven part of her that desperately wanted something more.

No. It didn't matter what she wanted it.

She couldn't have it.

Chapter Six

Abigail had no idea if Minerva would be in the church Wednesday afternoon or not. What if the prim schoolteacher had decided that she couldn't teach Abigail to read?

That was a consequence that Abigail would have to face. If Minerva didn't show, Abigail would set up some sort of bartering arrangement with one of her customers. Roy Griffith, the proprietor of the Golden Star hotel, was one of her regulars. He was a businessman and Abigail was fairly certain he cared more for her than just the sex. He might help her.

On the surface, it wasn't that different than the arrangement that she had made with Minerva. It was an exchange of services for knowledge. Just instead of a dress, it would be a sex act.

The bundle she had tucked in the small basket with some provisions felt heavy—far heavier than the sheer layers of silk and cotton actually weighed. As a goodwill gesture, bringing Minerva two new pairs of drawers was a bad idea. Never mind that the woman desperately needed new underthings or that providing her with new clothes was their deal. At the very least, if Minerva refused to continue with their lessons, that would be an even exchange, wouldn't it? One pair of drawers per lesson?

No doubt, the prim, severe spinster would look at the drawers in the same way that she had looked at Abigail right after she had pushed her away. Right after the softest of kisses.

She shouldn't have kissed Minerva. What had she been thinking?

Clearly, she hadn't been. Minerva hid herself away behind her prickly attitude and her terrible clothes. But underneath all of that, she was a warm, flesh-and-blood woman, lovely and kind. Kind enough to take on private tutoring with a soiled dove such as Abigail, anyway.

That something was warm and tender and it called to Abigail. Her life now was much better than it had been before, even considering she spread her legs every night. At least she controlled that, not the other way around. But even though she was safe and secure, there was still so little tenderness in it. And fool that she was, she had thought she could share that tenderness with someone like Minerva Krenshaw.

With a heavy heart, she climbed the stairs into the balcony of the Methodist Church. As she gained the second floor, she saw Minerva. Her heart leapt because at least Abigail would have the chance to offer up her apologies.

That, however, was not going to be easy. Minerva had never looked so severe—and that was saying something because she always looked severe. Everything about her today was buttoned up and closed off—which was only reinforced when she said, "Miss Whithall."

So that was how it was going to be. "Miss Krenshaw." She opened her mouth to ask how Minerva was doing today, but the older woman slanted

57

her a hard look and she thought better of it. "Thank you for meeting me today."

Minerva sniffed. "We had an agreement and I, for one, honor my agreements."

There was censure in that statement, but for the life of her Abigail couldn't quite figure out what it was. "About what happened last time—"

Minerva held up a hand. "We shall not speak of it, Miss Whithall. We are here to further your education—nothing more and nothing less."

That didn't seem right. How could Abigail *not* apologize? "But I need to say I'm sorry." And then she realized what Minerva had said. The teacher was going to keep teaching. She would not punish Abigail for her mistake. Her heart grew lighter. "I am most grateful that you are willing to continue teaching me and I promise that I will not overstep my bounds again."

At that, all of Minerva's severity fell away and Abigail could see that she was struggling. "You... won't?"

Was Abigail imagining it or was there a hint of regret in that question? "Of course not. I know my station and I feel terrible that I put you in a position where you felt you could not..." It was her turn to have the words trail off as she tried to find a way to say what she needed to say. "I wouldn't want to make you uncomfortable. You must know that I think highly of you and that you are lovely woman. I am forever grateful that you are still willing to teach me. I..." She might as well get this over with. Minerva was standing there, her mouth open in shock. "I made these. For you. You need them." Awkwardly, she pulled the bundle out of the basket and held it out.

It was an odd thing, to watch Minerva pull herself together. The confusion went first, followed by the shock. Each emotion was replaced with one of cold distance. "What is it? It's far too small to be a dress."

All things considered, this was going as well as one could hope. "It's some underthings." She would've thought that, at this point in her life, she was far past the ability to be embarrassed but she was. "I started on the dress, but I had some extra fabric and these were easy to whip up."

Minerva did not reach out her hand to take the small bundle wrapped in muslin and tied with a string. Instead, a long, painful silence stretched between them and Abigail once again considered the fact that Minerva just might damn her to hell for all of her many, many sins.

She was miserable. She had survived worse—but none of that had ever been because of her doing. She'd been born enslaved and freed only after tragedy had struck. She'd accepted an apprenticeship with Mr. Dawson because he had been a friend of Mrs. Whithall's and had promised to help her learn everything she'd needed to open her own shop, but those had all been clever lies designed to get her alone in his quarters.

No, her life up until this moment had been about weathering the worst that God could throw at her. And perhaps He had thrown Miss Minerva Krenshaw at her. No one had made Abigail kiss this woman. No one had forced her to dig her fingers into her hips and feel Minerva's flesh under her palms. She had done that of her own accord and now she would pay the price.

"Set them aside," Minerva said, her voice shaking. With fear? With disgust? Abigail couldn't tell. "We are here to learn to read. Everything else has to wait."

Wasn't that an interesting turn of phrase? But Abigail didn't dare smile. "Yes, of course. I practiced my name some more and I studied the letters in the reader you gave me."

Minerva sniffed again, but Abigail thought that perhaps she looked pleased by this. "You have been quite busy."

"Idle hands are the Devil's workshop."

There was another stunned pause and then Minerva's lips twitched into something that looked dangerously close to a smile. "Quite true. Shall we get started?"

*

Minerva had found herself musing about Abigail as she moved through her day. The girl really was quite smart. And that was something of a problem because it was bad enough that Abigail was beautiful, refined and cultured. It was worse that she had a talent with the needle. Minerva was almost afraid to open the little bundle that held the drawers—drawers, of all things! Abigail had a head for business and a drive to succeed, all admirable qualities.

But somehow, the fact that she was also intelligent felt like the proverbial straw that was going to break the camel's back. And, in this scenario, Minerva was the camel.

By the end of the lesson, Abigail could not only

write both of her names—a real one and her Jewel name—with a clean, even hand, but she was already able to pick out simple words from the reader. And worst of all, she apparently spoke French. French! Minerva didn't even speak French and she was an educated woman.

All of that was potentially damaging to Minerva's self-restraint. But the thing that absolutely did her in was how sincerely Abigail had apologized. In that moment, she had not been a cultured, refined woman of ill repute. She had not seemed confident at all.

Instead, her awkward, bumbling apology felt much more familiar to Minerva. It was almost as if neither of them knew quite what they were doing and that was reassuring, somehow.

Not that any of that mattered. It didn't. Minerva had taken Abigail's apology at face value. What happened last time would not happen again. It was simply that…simple.

"No m…man?" Abigail read in a halting, unsteady voice. Then she looked up from the reader for Minerva's approval. "Did I get it right?"

And there was such hopefulness in the girl's face that even though she knew she shouldn't, Minerva couldn't help but return that smile.

"Very good. You shall be reading in no time at all."

Abigail's whole face lit up. "I have a good teacher."

Oh, heavens. Where was her willpower? Where was her inner fortitude? She managed to sit back, putting precious inches between her and her student. It wasn't much in terms of resisting, but it counted for something. Hopefully.

Abigail looked away. "Will we continue our lessons?" She sounded nervous about that.

"Of course. If you can get a newspaper, see if you can pick out words you know and keep working on sounding out bigger words with the smaller words you recognize." There. That was a perfectly appropriate thing for her to say.

The color on Abigail's cheeks deepened ever so slightly. "Are we done with our lessons today?"

Minerva was so tempted to say *no* because if they were, that meant that she would either have to stay here and talk about clothing and dresses and drawers and measurements or flee like the coward that she really was. "We are," she heard herself say. No, no, *no*! She should—she should make Abigail practice her penmanship some more. She should insist that they start the next lesson in the reader. She should—

She should do anything but sit here, once again powerless, and stare in fascination as Abigail plucked the string tied around the muslin bundle to reveal silky white fabric.

"I had some extra fabric, so I made you two pairs," Abigail said as if this were the most normal conversation in the world instead of a discussion of intimate garments in the balcony of a church. "One pair is a more sturdy cotton and will last you a great long time. But the other is a softer fabric and I think you'll like how it feels against your..." she cleared her throat. "Skin."

The color on Abigail's cheeks deepened until true red showed through her creamy brown skin. She was a soiled dove. She flipped up her skirts for money. And yet, somehow, there could be something innocent about her.

It was dangerous to think of Abigail as somehow innocent or inexperienced. It was dangerous for Minerva to think she had anything in common with this young woman at all. Especially in physical matters.

Oh, but they weren't just drawers. Abigail held up a pair and shook it out and Minerva saw that the girl had sewn lace around the legs of the drawers. Lace! Minerva hadn't had an item of clothing embellished with lace in years. The scrap she had tried to sew to her bonnet was the very last piece she'd had when she left home.

No one would ever see these drawers. No one would ever know that Minerva was wearing such a fine garment with such fine lace.

"I wanted you to feel pretty in them," Abigail said, draping them over the back of the pew and holding up the second pair—the finer of the two. It shimmered in the light.

It was a waste of good lace. She needed to tell Abigail that. She needed to remind the girl that their deal was for a dress, not underthings. Never mind that Minerva's drawers were little more than rags with a drawstring through them. Never mind that there was a part of her that looked at those delicate underthings and wanted them.

Vanity was a sin.

So why couldn't she tell Abigail that?

Because it would be ungrateful. "They are beautiful," she whispered, reaching out and tentatively stroking a finger over the fine fabric.

The air around her seemed to take on a heated, heavy feel, like a storm rolling across the plains. She looked up to find Abigail stretched out so that she was as close to reclining as a body could get on the hard wooden pew in a Methodist Church and, on her face, she wore a dreamy smile as she watched Minerva finger the delicate fabric.

A deep sense of longing hit her low and deep and threatened to double her over. The last time they had met, Abigail had kissed her—and Minerva had pushed her away. She'd *had* to—there was no other choice but to refuse anything physical. She was Minerva Krenshaw. She had a reputation and a position to uphold. She could not...

Well, she simply could *not*.

"Then they suit you," Abigail said, her words soft and languid—a bedroom voice and a bedroom accent.

"I'm not. Pretty, that is." Even when she had been young and fresh, she had not been pretty.

Abigail sat up and unpacked the small basket she had brought with her. She produced a Mason jar and a small bundle wrapped in a handkerchief. "Sweet tea? I brought some sugar cookies, too."

Sweet tea? Cookies? This was doubly unfair. Minerva's mouth began to water and her willpower was nothing but a distant memory. "You didn't have to bring tea."

Oh, the cookies were dusted with sugar, the little crystals catching the light. How long had it been since Minerva had had something sweet? Sugar was dear, far more than she could afford on her salary.

Abigail held one out to her, an expectant look on her face. "I didn't make them," she said almost shyly. "But they're very good. Have one." When Minerva hesitated, Abigail added, "I brought them for you."

"Why would you do that?" But the moment the words left her mouth, she felt ungrateful. "I mean... Thank you. I'm not used to having..." But she couldn't even bring herself to say *having people do nice things for me* because it made her sound pitiful and sad and she didn't want to be pitiful or sad with Abigail. "Cookies. I'm not used to having cookies."

Unfortunately, that was still pretty pitiful.

"That's a shame," Abigail said, unscrewing the jar and taking a sip of the tea. "You should have some sweetness in your life. Tea? I'm sorry I couldn't grab any cups." She lowered her chin and then looked up at Minerva through her thick black lashes. "I hope it's all right if we share?"

Almost as if she had no control over her own self, Minerva leaned forward and put her lips to the edge of the jar. Gently, Abigail tilted the jar and the sweet tea hit her tongue like a kiss.

After so long of doing without, the decadence almost overwhelmed her. But she couldn't help herself. She drank deeply. Maybe she would never be able to help herself again.

"I do not expect you to serve me." Abigail's brows knit together and Minerva felt like a dunce. *Again.* "But it is very good and I thank you."

Abigail moved back so that she was reclining again. Minerva refused to look at her legs. But out of the corner of her eye, she could see that Abigail's skirt had ridden up and her ankles and her calves were visible.

"Can I ask you a question?"

"Of course. Questioning is one of the best ways to learn." Minerva nibbled at a cookie and the buttery sweetness melted in her mouth. Unwillingly, she let out a little moan of pleasure. "Oh, my."

"What happened the first time?"

Minerva snapped to attention immediately, almost choking on her cookie. "I don't know what you're talking about."

Abigail tilted her head, seemingly perfectly at ease. "For an intelligent woman, you say that a great deal. Did you know that? But I think you do."

"I assure you I do not." And then Minerva stuffed an entire cookie into her mouth so that she would be unable to politely respond to this most improper of questions.

"I can guess."

Minerva got very still. She willed her body to rise and her feet to carry her away from this place, this woman. But nothing moved.

"There was someone you cared for. Perhaps you even loved that person. And there came a day when they said or did something that made you think that they cared for you, too."

Minerva squeezed her eyes shut, but it didn't block out the words.

"And an opportunity presented itself, didn't it? You were sitting close together, just like we are now and... And you couldn't stop yourself from leaning forward and pressing your lips against the other person's."

It all came back to her. Every painful second of that most painful memory that she had put away years ago was suddenly fresh and new again. She had bought a pretty length of lace almost the exact same violet hue as Eliza's eyes. It was a birthday present and Eliza had looked so pleased with it. She had lifted her hair aside so that Minerva could tie the lace around her slender neck and then Eliza had turned back to Minerva and hugged her tightly, whispering that it was the very best gift anyone had ever given her.

And then Minerva had ruined everything. All for a single kiss.

"Yes," Abigail said softly, her voice closer now. Minerva did not dare open her eyes. "And this other person, they did not take the kiss in the spirit in which it was given, did they?"

"No," Minerva whispered.

Eliza's eyes had widened and then she shoved Minerva so hard that she had stumbled and fallen on her bottom. Minerva had tried to apologize, but she had been struck dumb as Eliza had ripped that pretty violet lace from her neck and thrown it down at Minerva's feet. And the things she had said...

"You poor woman. She was wrong, you know."

Of course Abigail knew. She was too smart not to have seen this particular truth. The truth that no one else had ever seen, much less guessed at. Eliza was the only other person.

"I can't do this," Minerva said, her voice shaking. "I'm not like you."

Even though she still had her eyes squeezed shut, she could feel the tension rolling off Abigail. "And how am I?"

Even if she didn't want to see, Minerva opened her eyes and looked at the young woman before her. She could see the worry tightening her body. "You know things. *Secret* things."

One corner of Abigail's mouth quirked up. "That is common knowledge. I would be happy," she added, "to answer any questions you might have. After all, questioning is one of the best ways to learn about anything, is it not?"

Even though she wanted to be anywhere but here having any conversation but this one, Minerva could not help it. She laughed. "You would throw my own words back at me, would you?"

"Oh," Abigail exhaled, that warm smile taking hold of her lips and making her look simply irresistible. She pressed a palm to her own bosom, as if she could barely contain herself. "You really should laugh more, Minerva."

It shouldn't matter that the girl had complimented her. Or brought her cookies and tea. Or sewn her the finest drawers that Minerva had ever seen. None of it should matter.

But it all did.

"I could not possibly ask any questions *here*."

Abigail thought about this for a moment. "It will be several more weeks before I have a dress ready for a fitting. I do not think it would be wise if we did that here again. That made you very uncomfortable."

Minerva gave her a dull look. That wasn't what had sent her running. "I don't know where you think we would meet otherwise. I could not possibly be seen going into the Jeweled Ladies and you could not possibly be seen coming into the schoolhouse. To take a room at the hotel would be equally impossible. The entire situation is *impossible*."

Abigail's eyes lit up. "You've thought about a room, then?"

Minerva had. All of those rooms, all with beds. Lacy drawers and sweet tea—it was all madness.

But as she looked at Abigail, she didn't see the same censure that she had seen in Eliza's eyes. She didn't see the disgust, the anger. She only saw warmth and honesty and curiosity. And as she looked, she could feel her resolution wavering.

Would it be so bad, to ask? She understood the mechanics of intercourse between men and women. She assumed it was roughly the same as the mechanics of intercourse between dogs or horses. But how did two women do *anything*?

She could feel her cheeks heating just at the thought. And as Abigail's smile deepened, Minerva knew that the girl could see the blush, too.

"Let's not think of it now," Abigail said, sitting up and putting the tea things back in the small basket. "For now, let's just focus on the lessons. I will figure something out when it's time for your dress fitting."

Two distinct emotions took up arms against each other inside Minerva's chest. Was Abigail truly not going to try to kiss her again? Good. Minerva certainly did not want to be kissed again.

But even thinking such things in a house of God—even if that house was Methodist—was surely a sin because God himself would know that it was a lie and that Minerva was disappointed that Abigail was smoothing her skirts and pinning her hat back on top of her artfully piled hair and, in general, looking beautiful and graceful.

"Yes," she agreed, picking up her own bonnet. The scrap of faded violet lace caught her eye. "We shall focus on the lessons."

She would not think about the kiss—any kiss. She would put the pain of Eliza's rejection back in the little box she kept it in and she would put the hope of Abigail's soft touches and easy laughter away, as well.

Hope was a dangerous thing and she could not indulge in it.

"Shall I bring tea next time, as well?" Abigail asked.

"We should take turns. Except…"

Except Minerva had very little tea and no sugar and butter only some of the time, when one of her students brought her some.

Abigail opened her mouth and Minerva thought the girl might offer to pay her for the lessons—with her ill-gotten money. And then Minerva would have to refuse again, as if her poverty were point of pride.

"Our next lesson is tomorrow. I will not be able to linger, so it won't be necessary."

The reminder that Abigail would leave this church and return to that brothel was painful. How was Minerva going to get through this with her dignity and decency intact?

"Then perhaps I shall get here a little earlier," she said. "I should not want to deprive you of your lessons."

It was a foolish statement to make, but when Abigail gave her that wide smile, she couldn't regret it. "Then I shall see you early." Abigail left first, but she paused at the top of the stairs and threw a lingering look back over her shoulder to Minerva.

This time, instead of racing home to hide her tears, Minerva all but floated on a cloud of something that felt a great deal like happiness.

Chapter Seven

Two and a half weeks passed. In that time, Abigail and Minerva met another eight times. Abigail didn't want to say that learning to read was easy—because if it was, then she should have been able to do it earlier. But it was certainly *easier* with Minerva sitting next to her, patiently walking her through each pronunciation and spelling.

Back when they'd been children, Miss Catherine had done everything possible to avoid doing her studies. They'd gone through several governesses, much to Mrs. Whithall's dismay. Governesses were not cheap and they only had a little money left to them after Mr. Whithall's passing. But Mrs. Whithall had been determined that her daughter would be a proper lady who'd catch the eye of a prosperous, attractive gentleman. So she had paid for the governesses.

Abigail had always been jealous of that. She had loved Miss Catherine dearly, as a sister and a friend. Miss Catherine had loved her, too. During the dark time after the Whithalls had succumbed to the fever and Abigail had been trapped by Mr. Dawson, knowing that she had been Miss Catherine's and Miss Catherine had been hers had been maybe the only thing that saved her sanity—that and the dream of her shop. She *knew* that there was love and light and happiness in the world, even for enslaved girls who couldn't read.

But Abigail had expected reading to be harder. Miss Catherine had always thrown tantrums when it came to her studies. In Abigail's mind, that meant that these were impossible mountains that one could never finish climbing—not something she would enjoy. Not something that would bear fruit in less than a month.

But it had. In less than four weeks, she was able to sit down with the newspaper and her morning cup of chocolate and, if not completely understand what was printed on the page, at the very least get the idea of it. Minerva had told her to keep a list of words she came across that she didn't know and they then spent part of every lesson going over these words.

Sometimes, she wrote down words just to listen to Minerva define them for her. When she taught, her face lost some of its severity and she made big gestures with her hands. This was who Minerva was when she wasn't trying so hard to be the dowdy schoolmarm. Abigail could watch her for hours.

They made a great deal of progress in a month. Minerva focused on phrases that Abigail would need for her business, so Abigail would routinely write sentences such as, "The brown dress will cost twelve dollars and fifty cents, but the blue dress will cost fourteen dollars."

And over that month, Abigail would bring tea and cookies and small cakes, sometimes sandwiches if Della had a few extra. Minerva would always protest that it was unfair that Abigail provided the afternoon tea. She should contribute as well. She would remind Abigail that she did not expect to be served by her students.

72

Abigail had asked around. Other students would bring in things for the teacher—a quart of cream, a fresh-baked pie. It was part of her pay, only not in dollars. So she did not feel bad about packing up a few sweets for her teacher. Besides, Minerva needed more sweetness in her life.

She had not kissed Minerva again. In fact, they had not so much as touched.

But there had been long looks over the slate. With each sip of sweet tea, Minerva smiled more. She got more comfortable with Abigail. She let herself laugh more.

Sometimes, when Abigail was working and pretending that she was enjoying the men pawing at her because they'd paid for that right, she lay back and thought about Minerva instead. The way her eyes lit up when Abigail pronounced a difficult word correctly. In fact, the only time they *had* touched had been when Abigail had read *chrysanthemum* correctly on the first try and Minerva had been so pleased that she had reached over and squeezed Abigail's hand.

Thoughts like that kept her going.

Through it all, she sewed dresses for Minerva. The fabric for the shift came in, but Abigail decided not to give it to Minerva in the church—but where? Minerva couldn't be seen going into the brothel and Abigail couldn't be seen going into the schoolhouse.

But what if she wasn't seen? Sometimes, people snuck into the Jeweled Ladies. Always with Mistress's permission, of course, but they did manage to find their way in. Why couldn't Abigail do the same thing?

What if she snuck into the schoolhouse?

*

The schoolhouse shone. In a fit of nervous energy, Minerva had scrubbed every surface until it gleamed. The floor was so shiny that it was difficult to look at it straight on. Every desktop was neat and orderly. And although there was no room to change in her little bedroom at the back of the house, Minerva had washed the sheets and made the bed. Not because she expected Abigail to do any more than maybe peek her head through the doorway and look at the meager room with a mixture of horror and dismay. No, it was decided. Abigail wouldn't even come back to this room.

Minerva made the bed twice.

She checked the watch on her chest again. Seven fifty-three—the seconds dragged by. At eight o'clock, Abigail was supposed to slink out of the fall darkness and into the schoolhouse. It was a cold night, with heavy clouds in the air. The moon was hidden and the weather threatened. Surely everyone would be home, snug in their beds.

Abigail had chosen Sunday night because they had rules at the Jeweled Ladies, and one of them was that the brothel did not entertain on Sundays. So it only made sense that Sunday would be the day when no one would come looking for either of them.

Just to be sure, Minerva made the bed a third time.

All that was going to happen was a dress fitting. Nothing but...

Minerva stripping down to her underthings and standing before Abigail. The dim light from her stove and lamp would render the shift completely see-through. There would be no hiding.

She was eyeing the bed for the fourth time and wondering if she should've put on the sturdy cotton drawers instead of the silky ones when a small knock came from the front of the schoolroom. Even though it was quiet, it still sounded like a gunshot to Minerva's ears. She all but ran to the door and threw the bolt back.

She'd been expecting Ebony White. Or, at the very least, Abigail Whithall. But what stood before her was a different sort of creature entirely—hunched over, wearing a grimy dress that looked huge, with a black shawl pulled up over its head and a cloak thrown over that for good measure.

"Hello?" What if this was not Abigail but was some poor, destitute creature looking for warmth on a cold night?

The figure straightened and Abigail's face beamed up at her. "Can I come in?"

Minerva all but yanked her into the schoolroom and slammed the door shut behind them. "Did anyone see you?"

Abigail began shedding the many, many layers she was wearing. "The Snyders were closing up the dry-goods store, so I asked them for directions to Free Franklin's place."

The room began to spin and Minerva sagged back against the door. "You spoke to the Snyders?"

Abigail paused and then shrank four inches before Minerva's eyes. "Oh, good sir," she crackled out in an aged voice that had such a thick southern accent that Minerva had trouble understanding her, "I heard tell there was a place for beggars like me?" But that was as far as she got before she threw her head back and began to laugh. "Trust me, Minerva, no one knew who I was."

Minerva wasn't sure, but she had to admit that she wouldn't have recognized Abigail. "What are you wearing?" Because it was disconcerting to see this woman, who was usually dressed in the height of fashion, wearing a dress that—well, was more like the ones that Minerva owned.

"A few of Della's castoffs," she said, unwinding a massive skirt from her hips and letting it fall to the floor.

It was like watching a butterfly emerge from a cocoon. Each layer Abigail stripped off got closer to revealing her true self. Finally, she stood before Minerva in a dress she'd never seen before. "I didn't think you owned things that weren't black."

Abigail shrugged. "That's one of Mistress's rules. We all have to dress in our colors at all times. I have other clothes and I figured it didn't matter tonight."

It was a cotton dress, simply cut but well-made, with a gentle flare at the hips. It didn't so much cling to Abigail's curves, not like her other dresses did, but it flattered her nonetheless. It was the color that made it remarkable, a deep blush that seems to bring out the roses in Abigail's cheeks.

Minerva couldn't do anything but stand there and blink at the girl. This, she realized, was the true Abigail Whithall. Something in her chest unclenched.

With that dreamy smile on her face, Abigail turned and took in the magnitude of the schoolroom. "I've never been in a school before," she said with a note of awe in her voice.

"A shame, that." Minerva managed to shove

herself away from the door. Now that Abigail was here, she saw a million things that she should have set to rights. She had missed sweeping out the far corner of the room. She should have moved her desk and mopped underneath it.

Abigail should not have come. Minerva wasn't ready for this.

"This is nice," Abigail said and indeed, she did sound impressed. "Where do you stay? Surely you don't have to sleep on a pallet by the stove—do you?" The way she said it, as if that were the most logical spot—Minerva had to wonder.

Minerva took a deep breath, glad she had made sure that the bed was properly made. "I have a little room through that door. But I'm sure it's not as grand as your room at the Jeweled Ladies."

"I wasn't always a Jewel, Minerva." She picked up the two baskets that she had carried in with her and began to head back toward the stove, where there was the most light. "The Whithall ladies were not well off. I was their only…help. And then…" She came to a halting stop as her words trailed off.

Minerva took a step toward her. She wanted to do something—put a hand on Abigail's shoulder to comfort her, wrap her arms around her and let her know she was not alone. *Something.*

But she couldn't and, after a second, Abigail shook herself. "Doesn't signify. Are you ready to try on your new dress?"

Abigail moved to the small space she'd cleared from the stove. "It does signify. What happened to you is important—but not as important as the fact that you're now free."

The girl looked up at her with wet eyes. "I don't like to talk about it." Minerva started to nod, but Abigail went on, "but if I did talk about it, it would be with you."

She couldn't help herself. She stepped close to Abigail and clasped her hands. "If you want to talk, I will always listen."

Abigail squeezed her fingers tight and then let them go. But she didn't turn away from Minerva. Instead, she stepped in closer. After the briefest of hesitations, she lifted her fingers to the buttons on Minerva's Sunday dress.

This time, instead of cataloguing all of the ways that this was a sin—although it still was—she just stood still while Abigail undid her buttons.

"I think you're going to be so pleased," Abigail whispered. There was no need to whisper. There was no risk of being overheard.

Minerva breathed deeply, letting the scents of lavender and vanilla wash over. Her fingers itched to settle around Abigail's waist and feel her soft flesh in her hands. But she was a rock. She could not move. To do so would be ruin.

"You're shaking," Abigail said, pushing the dress off her shoulders and down over her hips. To do this, she had bent down, her face only inches from Abigail's exposed bosom. "Are you cold?"

"No." Oh, how she wanted to touch Abigail's hair.

She almost did it, too. Her hand was moving when Abigail straightened. "Nervous?" she asked with a reassuring smile as Minerva stepped out of her dress and kicked it to the side.

78

No. Yes. "A little." Not like she had been the last time they had done this. This nervous energy was something entirely different. Something that made her breasts feel heavy and her stomach tighten.

"Don't be," Abigail said, her voice a sigh on the wind. "There's nothing wrong with any of this."

They were talking about a dress fitting, weren't they? Well, Minerva wasn't. Abigail had already kissed her once. Briefly and quietly. She had already stripped Minerva down to her underthings once, too.

Minerva was supposed to be above temptation.

Oh, but she was tempted.

That temptation only got stronger as Abigail undid the busks of Minerva's corset. "You must promise me never to wear this again," she said in a light, teasing tone.

"Then what shall I wear? Surely you're not suggesting I go without."

The busks gave and Minerva's breasts tightened even more as they were freed. And then, as bold as day, Abigail dropped her gaze down to Minerva's chest and that dreamy smile lifted the corners of her mouth. "I wouldn't mind."

Those three little words went off in Minerva's head like a firecracker. Feebly, she tried to remember all of the reasons why she was not allowed to fall in love with this girl. It was a sin. Abigail was a soiled dove. Minerva had a reputation to protect.

None of that mattered when Abigail leaned down and grabbed the hem of Minerva's shift. As she lifted it over Minerva's thighs, her hands stayed close. Minerva could feel the heat of her knuckles grazing over her hips and up her waist. Over the sides of her breasts and then Minerva was raising her hands and the shift was pulled free and all that was left were her stockings and her drawers. The soft, silky pair that Abigail had made just for her.

"Oh, Minerva, look at you." If it had been anyone else, Minerva would've been sure she was being mocked. But before she could say anything, Abigail stepped in closer, closer than she had yet been. Abigail's entire body leaned toward her. "You really are a lovely woman."

"I don't know how you can say that."

Somehow, her hands had come to rest on Abigail's waist and Abigail's arms were around her neck. Minerva had no memory of this happening, just that she was now holding this girl and this girl was holding her and it felt so, so *right*. "I can say it because it's true."

"But I'm nothing compared with all of those other Jewels. Nothing compared to you. You're the most beautiful girl I've ever seen."

There was a moment when their heads got closer together and Minerva could feel Abigail's sweet breath bouncing off her cheek. And then Abigail's hands were unraveling Minerva's tight braid. "You are lovely," she said as Minerva's hair came loose, pins scattering to the floor. "I wish you could see yourself as I see you."

Her hair fell like a curtain down her back. "How do you see me?" she heard herself ask.

Abigail ran her fingers through Minerva's hair, spreading it out over her shoulders. "I see your smile and your laugh. I see the way you teach me when no one else has. I see your kindness and your warm eyes.

I see the beauty you try so desperately to hide. You don't have to hide from me, Minerva. I like you a great deal and I hope that we can be…friends, in a fashion. Something more than student and teacher. Special *friends.*"

"This is wrong." It was a last-ditch attempt, but even as she said it, Minerva was lowering her lips to Abigail's.

"It doesn't have to be."

"I don't know anything." It was lowering to admit it.

Of course, the girl already knew this. "I can show you." Her lips brushed over Minerva's, the promise of a kiss to come. "If you want me to."

"You're only here for the dresses."

Abigail's hands spread wide across Minerva's bare back, sending flames of passion licking over her skin. Everything felt heavy and hot and it only got hotter when Abigail said, "No, I'm not."

Chapter Eight

This time, when Abigail kissed her, Minerva didn't push her away. Instead, she made little whimpering noises of helplessness and happiness, her fingers digging into Abigail's hips and pulling her in closer.

Finally, Abigail thought. After a month, she was *finally* going to get to explore Minerva.

Women are soft and wonderful creatures. That was what ran through Abigail's mind as Minerva's mouth softened for her. She had to move slowly because it would not take much to send Minerva running back for the cover of morality.

As it was, she could feel Minerva struggling. The woman was trembling so violently that it was a wonder she could keep her feet under her. The noises she made as Abigail kissed and licked and stroked with her mouth veered dangerously close to cries of pain.

But for all of that, Minerva did not break the kiss. Abigail wondered at the glory of it. Mistress had been right—Abigail always enjoyed her time with Opal. Certainly more than she enjoyed taking men to bed.

But this? This wasn't an act she and Opal performed for someone else's pleasure. This was for her and Minerva. No one else—just them.

She kissed the corner of Minerva's mouth. "Show me," Minerva said in a voice that was little more than an exhale. "I want to know."

Abigail licked Minerva's lips and let her fingers stroke up and down her bare back. Minerva's muscles twitched and her mouth opened.

When she was working at the brothel, Abigail focused on pretending. Each sex act was a performance, one she was paid handsomely for. She had to be something other than she was. She liked being with Opal, but it wasn't for her, those kisses and touches. Always, it was for the man.

But this? Arousal and awareness coiled together low in her body, tightening her breasts and making her pussy wetter. She wasn't pretending as she dipped her tongue in Minerva's mouth and then retreated, giving her a moment to adjust to the intimacies.

Minerva had a clean, fresh taste—one of tooth powder that combined with the scent of lemons, instead of whiskey and cigar smoke. It wasn't overly sweet, but then again—neither was Minerva.

It was practically intoxicating and, as Minerva opened for her, Abigail began to lose herself in the kiss. She explored Minerva's mouth, tasting and touching and drinking Minerva in until she couldn't think straight.

"What should I do?" Minerva asked as she ran her palms over the sleeves of Abigail's dress. "Should I..."

Right. She was suddenly no longer the pupil, but the teacher. "Would you undo my buttons?" Abigail made sure to phrase it as a question. She didn't want to presume anything at this point.

Minerva bit her lip, but she nodded. Abigail turned and waited.

There was a brief hesitation and then she felt Minerva's hands on her, working the buttons. "I shouldn't be doing this."

"We can stop."

Minerva didn't reply. Not in words, anyway. She continued to undo the buttons on the back of Abigail's dress until the whole thing sagged. Abigail shimmied out of it and then bent over to pick it up and shake it out. She was rather fond of that dress and didn't want it wrinkled.

As she did so, Minerva gasped. "I—you—"

Abigail turned and smiled. "I don't like drawers. Although I like seeing you in them."

Minerva stood as if frozen and Abigail let her look. It was entirely possible that she had never seen another woman in her underthings. Abigail had worn her finest shift, one that was so thin and gauzy that it was practically see-through.

She had made her own corset—black, of course. It came to just under her nipples and put her bosom on its best display. She wore no drawers, only sheer silk stockings imported from Paris.

Minerva's mouth hung open, a hand pressed against her chest as she took in everything.

If she were working, Abigail would be forcing herself to ignore the heavy weight in her stomach, forcing herself to smile and bat her eyelashes. She'd be telling herself that she could do this, she could get through another night. She would think about the money she was making, about the little shop full of bolts of fabric and pins and needles and the big worktable for cutting out patterns. She would spread her legs and think about shelves of fashion plates and spools of lace and taking a woman much like Minerva and transforming her into something *more* with just the right cut of fabric. She would do that again and again until she had made it through another night and put another twenty or thirty dollars into her bank account.

But tonight? As Minerva stood there in her drawers and stockings, Abigail didn't have any of those feelings of awfulness. Instead, her heart was pounding and the only thing she could think about was that she hoped this woman wouldn't suddenly change her mind.

She began to work the laces of her corset loose. "Have you ever seen another woman nude before?"

Minerva didn't answer, not in words. Some of the shock was fading from her eyes and, as the corset gave, a new emotion began to take hold—one that Abigail recognized all too well. *Lust.* Which was a relief because Abigail had not read the situation wrong. Instead, everything was very, very right.

Then she went to grab the hem of her shift and lift it over her head, but the most wonderful thing happened—Minerva moved in and said, "Let—let me. If that's okay?"

"This is your first time? With anyone?" She hoped so. It seemed clear that Minerva had no taste for men and Abigail could only pray that no one had ever forced her. There should still be some innocence in this world.

Minerva nodded, a high blush reddening her cheeks.

"The most important thing to remember," Abigail said, reaching out and stroking her fingertips over Minerva's bare shoulders, "is to tell me what you like and what you don't like."

"But I don't know what I don't like. I don't know what I'm doing!"

Frustration was not erotic. So Abigail did the only thing she could think of—she kissed Minerva again, harder this time. "You're already doing it," she whispered against Minerva's lips before she plunged her fingers back in to her silky hair and took her mouth over and over.

She didn't think of dress shops or fabrics or pattern books. All Abigail could think, feel, taste was Minerva. Minerva grabbed her shift and yanked it over her head and then put her hands on Abigail's body as their mouths found each other again and again. Minerva hesitantly cupped one of Abigail's breasts. Abigail moaned encouragingly—which made Minerva drop her hand away as if she had picked up something hot.

"It's okay," Abigail whispered. "It felt good. I want to touch you like that, too."

"Is it—I mean—" Minerva's hand closed around her left breast again, testing the weight. "I want…"

"Tell me."

Minerva's back arched, the hard nubs of her breasts pointed in Abigail's direction. "I want you to touch me."

"Good. That's good." Minerva was going to need all the encouragement she could get.

She traced her fingertips over the tops of Abigail's bare breasts, watching her already tight nipples tighten even more. "Look how pretty you are," she said as she pressed her lips against Minerva's neck.

"Not as pretty as you are." As she said it, Minerva brought her hand up and rested it on the top of Abigail's head. "I don't know… About your hair…"

Abigail looked up at her. "You can muss up my hair. I already mussed up yours."

That was the right thing to say. Minerva smiled—perhaps not the wide, confident smile of a woman who was about to get what she wanted in bed, but she smiled nonetheless. Abigail turned her attention back to her breasts. She kept her touches light as she backed Minerva up so that the woman was leaning against the edge of her desk and then she was half sitting on it. Which was good—it gave Abigail more to work with.

She stroked and teased and finally swept her thumbs over the tight tips. Minerva's head fell back as she groaned with pleasure. "Do you like that?" Abigail asked, nudging Minerva's knees apart with her leg and stepping in between. Heat rolled off her center and the smell of sex hung heavy in the air.

Minerva had one hand buried in Abigail's hair and the other gripped tightly on her shoulder. "Oh God," she said, her voice high and tight with need just as her nipples were high and tight under Abigail's relentless touches.

"Have you ever shattered, Minerva?" she asked, sweeping her thumbs over both nipples and then kissing along the tops of the breasts. "Have you ever touched yourself at night and thought of a beautiful girl?"

"Shattered?" she asked, her voice wavering.

No, then. "Oh, my darling woman, you have *so* much to learn."

With that, Abigail lowered her mouth to Minerva's breast and began to suckle. Her flesh was hot and as Abigail flicked her tongue back over the tight bud of the nipple, Minerva began to rise against her, her breath coming hotter and faster, her noises getting louder and more needy.

"Abigail," she gritted out through clenched teeth. "I don't—oh, *God.*"

"I've got you. Let it come."

"I need—I need—I don't know *what* I need," Minerva wailed, but even as the words left her mouth, her hips angled toward Abigail.

Abigail smiled. Minerva might not know what she needed, but her body did. She slid her hands between Minerva's legs, stroking her inner thighs through the soft fabric of the nicer pair of drawers. "Did you wear the fancy pair just for me?"

"I wanted to be pretty for you."

Abigail lifted her head and slid a hand back behind Minerva's neck so that the woman had nowhere else to look. "You are beautiful, Minerva. Don't ever let anyone tell you you're not—not even yourself." And then she touched the tight bud of Minerva's sex through the drawers.

She gasped in surprise as her hips bucked, but Abigail didn't let her go. She merely held still and gave Minerva a chance to adjust to the new sensation.

A strange sort of possessiveness took hold of Abigail. This was Miss Minerva Krenshaw—the iciest woman in town and right now, Abigail had her sprawled out on the top of her desk, panting and begging.

Abigail ran her finger over the seam at the center of the drawers, learning where Minerva needed her touch most. Abigail took care of everything. She sucked and licked Minerva's nipples gently as her fingers worked against the peak of Minerva's pussy. She longed to thrust a finger into Minerva's wet heat, to taste her tart sweetness.

Minerva, she learned, did not have the guile to be quiet. "Oh God," she moaned as Abigail pushed her body higher and higher.

And then Minerva came apart in her arms. Her back arched and her legs clamped around Abigail's hips and she made a high, keening noise in the back of her throat. Then it was over as she collapsed back onto the desk, panting and hauling Abigail down into her arms. "Oh my *God*," she murmured again and again.

Abigail kissed where she could—Minerva's chest, her neck, her chin, her lips. "So very pretty," she murmured as Minerva's body went limp with satisfaction.

Abigail was bent over at the waist and Minerva couldn't be comfortable with the bare wood digging into her backside. But they lay like that together for long moments.

"Was that all right?" she finally asked, her voice shaking.

Abigail laughed. "You were perfect."

Minerva's arms came around Abigail shoulders again. "But I didn't do any of that to you," she said, sounding worried and full of wonder at the same time.

"No, you didn't." But the heavy weight between her legs only got heavier at the thought of Minerva's hands sliding between her legs, stroking over her swollen bud and maybe even up into her pussy. "But that wasn't everything."

Minerva's head popped up. "It wasn't?"

Abigail laughed again, pushing herself back and hauling Minerva up into a sitting position. "My darling woman, that was only the beginning."

Chapter Nine

Only the beginning?" Minerva gaped at Abigail, unable to process the words. She wasn't even sure she was still breathing.

A word kept trying to bubble up to the front of her mind—*shattered*? Wasn't that what Abigail had asked right before she had—she had—

Well. Right before she *had*.

It wasn't a bad word. Minerva tested it out again. *Shattered*. It would do, she decided. But it wasn't quite right because Minerva didn't feel like she had broken, not like a crock dropped on the ground. More like...she had turned inside out and been spun upside down and then the whole process reversed and now she supposed she looked the same but she would never, ever *feel* the same. How could she go back to what she had been before?

Because she knew now. All those years ago when she had kissed Eliza, that bliss was what she had been chasing.

She was shaking with relief, with want, with the need for more. Shouldn't there be more? "I want to do that for you. Will you help me?"

Abigail looked up at her through thick lashes. She was the most beautiful girl Minerva had ever seen.

"How could I say no? Maybe we could move somewhere else?"

Minerva nodded. "The bed will be cold."

"It won't stay cold for long," Abigail said with a knowing smile. She pulled Minerva to her feet and slid her arms around her waist.

A nervous laugh bubbled out between Minerva's lips. Maybe this was just a dream? The most vivid, satisfying dream of her entire life. But then, if it were, she would hope she would have the imagination to dream of a fine room with a warm fire in a big, soft bed instead of the narrow, straw-filled mattress.

Abigail turned to her and Minerva was kissing her back and she stopped thinking about the room. Abigail's mouth was sweet on hers, her hands warm as they stroked over Minerva's skin. Minerva tried to do the same. She cupped Abigail's breasts, so much larger than hers. Abigail's nipples were darker, too, and much wider. Minerva remembered that Abigail had kissed her there and so, experimentally, she lowered her head and swiped her tongue across the dark nipple.

"Good," Abigail said, which was reassuring. But not as reassuring as the way her voice wavered ever so slightly. Was that desire?

Abigail plucked at the drawstring on the pretty drawers and they fell to the ground. Even though Minerva wanted to take the lead, it was Abigail who rolled down her stockings and did the same to Minerva's. It was Abigail who pushed Minerva onto the bed and covered her body. It was Abigail who was doing most of the touching and caressing.

It wasn't fair. Abigail shouldn't be doing all of

this—even if she was doing it quite well. The pressures that had peaked when Minerva had shattered were building again. But she wanted to make Abigail shatter, too. She was nothing if not fair. "Wait—I should be—"

"You are," Abigail replied and then she took Minerva's hand and cupped it to her breast. "Pinch the tip between your thumb and forefinger—but gently."

Minerva did as she was instructed and was rewarded with a low, soft moan from Abigail's lips.

"Yes, like that," Abigail whispered, and then she was rolling onto her back and Minerva was propped up along her side, running her hands up and down her body, from her shoulder to her breast to her waist to her hips—to her inner thighs.

"Like this?"

"Anywhere you want to touch me is good." Abigail said once again as she buried her hands into Minerva's hair. "Anywhere you want to *kiss* me is good."

She didn't mean…anywhere?

No, surely not. Instead, she kissed Abigail's lips and neck and chest. Especially that part. She let her tongue linger over the dark nipples and then sucked them into her mouth like a brazen hussy. Abigail moaned again, a deeper sound this time, and Minerva gave herself over to the sweet taste of this girl. Here, lying on this bed with this girl in her arms, Minerva was the kind of wanton, shameless woman she had never allowed herself to even imagine.

She would've been content with all of this—but Abigail had earlier touched her between her legs and made her world turn inside out. So she let her hands

93

trace up and down from the inside of Abigail's knees to the top of her hips. Abigail's legs fell open and she murmured, "Yes," into Minerva's hair. "Oh, I want you to touch me so bad. Only you."

She ran her hands over the soft hair that covered the place where Abigail's legs met. Abigail guided Minerva's fingers down until she could feel a hot, throbbing nub of flesh. Abigail gasped in pleasure when Minerva pressed against that little nub. "Yes, Minerva—oh, *yes*."

"I want to see." Knowledge is power and she didn't know anything about a woman's pleasure and where it was seated. But she wanted to. More than anything in her entire life, she wanted to know *everything*.

Abigail's grip on her hair lessened. She shifted so that her feet were pressed against the bed and her knees bent, her legs spread wide. "Come to me," she murmured in that dreamy voice.

So Minerva did. She climbed between Abigail's legs and sat back on her heels, studying the perfection of this girl. She explored with her hands, marveling at the softness of the skin on her inner thighs, the warmth from the little nub she had touched earlier.

This part of a woman—Minerva had been raised to think of it as improper. When she had gotten her courses for the first time, her mother had whispered to her what was happening in a room with the curtains drawn. This part of Minerva's body was not to be seen or touched except for the most basic cleanings. When she was married, her mother had explained, her husband would know what to do.

But Minerva would *never* marry. She'd always

known that, but here? Lying in bed with this delicious girl? No, she would never share her bed with a man.

As Abigail lay spread wide for her, Minerva waited for that feeling of shame to creep back in. As she studied Abigail, she could not find that shame. All she could feel was that same sense of inside-out happiness she had earlier. It was weaker now, more like an urge building inside of her. "I never knew you could be this beautiful."

Abigail watched Minerva, her breath coming in fast little pants. "Questions? You must have some."

"How do you like to be touched?"

Abigail's lips curved into a secret smile. "You know what? No one's ever asked me that before."

"Well, I'm asking." Abigail shifted again and a new scent overlaid the ones of vanilla and lavender. Minerva couldn't describe it, but there was something to it that called to her. Something deep and earthy and Abigail.

"Put your hand here at the top of my pussy and then kiss me. Always kiss me."

Blushing at the improper word, Minerva did as she was told. Abigail's flesh was warm and wet beneath her hand and her hand moved through that wetness as she leaned forward and laid her mouth to Abigail's and tried to find relief for the tension that was already coiling inside of her again.

This was nothing like she had seen dogs and horses do. But it felt right all the same. Their mouths moved everywhere, together and separately and then together again. Abigail began to pant into her, her hips shifting from side to side. "Oh God, Minerva—yes," she gasped when Minerva's hands slipped and her fingers sank into Abigail's warm wetness. "You can touch me there."

"Where?" Minerva asked, suddenly confused.

Abigail rolled slightly toward her. "Here. I'll show you." And then her fingers were stroking over Minerva's pussy, as she had so boldly called it, stroking lower, and then moving higher, a finger slipping inside of Minerva.

Minerva's back came off the bed. It was too much and not enough and oh, God, she really was going to die of happiness. "Oh, you beautiful woman," Abigail whispered against her neck. "I can feel your muscles. Oh God, I'm going to come. Here—right here." With her other hand, she covered Minerva's fingers and pressed them against that little nub, that secret place. And then everything about her went tight in Minerva's arms and Minerva's body responded in kind. The world turned inside out and upside down as Abigail cried out and Minerva did the same.

And then they were a tangle of arms and legs, both breathing hard. Minerva pulled Abigail against her chest and marveled as their bodies went soft against each other. "I had no idea," Minerva murmured into Abigail's hair. "I just had *no* idea."

Abigail laughed, a gentle sound of pure happiness. It did not feel like she was making fun of Minerva. Instead, it felt comforting. "Think of it as learning how to read. Today you learn how to recognize words. If you want, we can practice on stringing together sentences and whole paragraphs."

If Minerva wanted? What kind of question was that?

"But I don't want you to feel obligated," Abigail

went on before Minerva could find any words, spoken or otherwise, to string together into a single sentence. "I know this won't be easy for you."

"Is it easy for you?"

Abigail looked at her, brushing a strand of her hair out of Minerva's face. "Being with you is incredibly easy, Minerva. I like you—a great deal. Believe me when I say that I don't like what I do or the people I do it with."

Minerva frowned at that. "Then why do you do it?"

Abigail shrugged as if whoring herself was just one of those things. Then she sat up and, in the dim light, Minerva saw something she hadn't noticed before.

Long, pale scars crisscrossed Abigail's back. Minerva gasped in horror. Maybe it wasn't a surprise that Abigail had been beaten. But to see the evidence broke Minerva's heart. "Who did that to you?"

Abigail spoke. "After the Whithalls died…"

Minerva moved without thinking. She pulled the girl down into her arms and pulled the covers up over them.

She had heard stories, back when her father was one of the last stops on the Underground Railroad. Slave women—and men—would come through and tell their tales to the first willing ear, as if saying the words out loud would somehow help make the horrors of enslavement dissipate into the evening air as her mother fed the runaways a hearty meal and her father readied the wagon with the false bottom.

People who owned another human were abhorrent. Some of them may have been more kindly than others, and some were definitely worse, but they were all abhorrent excuses for Christians—for humans.

The worst ones, though, left the biggest scars. She had heard hair-raising tales of masters who held the enslaved in sexual dungeons, who subjected them to horrors too awful to mention.

It was the realization that Abigail had probably lived through something very similar that made Abigail's heart hurt for the woman. "It's okay. You don't have to say if you don't want to."

"I only do this because it's the quickest way to get to my shop," Abigail said after several long moments. "Otherwise, I'd get a job as a maid, and it might take the rest of my life to earn enough money. Colored maids don't earn much, you know. And I'd be at the mercy of my employers. What's to say the husband wouldn't decide to force me anyway? *No*."

Minerva held the dear girl tightly. There was a certain measure of sense to her words but still… "You could have tried to get an apprenticeship."

Her shoulders sagged. "I did." She waved a hand over her shoulder. "And he left me with those."

Minerva gasped in horror. "What happened?"

Abigail was silent for a moment before she shook her head and said, "It doesn't signify."

"It does," Minerva protested, but Abigail was having none of it.

"It doesn't matter," she said more firmly. "All that matters is what happens next. I want to be my own woman. And I don't ever want anyone to have control over me ever again. And I know you may not see the distinction, but I have a measure of control at the

Jeweled Ladies. I can say *no*. When I say *yes*, I am paid and paid well. I'd never been able to say no before and I was already ruined. Mistress buys me all the fabrics I want so almost everything I make goes right into my account. Maybe in another year, I'll have enough to move on and get that shop of mine."

A sense of hopelessness filled Minerva. She had nothing to offer this girl. She didn't have the means to buy her that shop now. Heavens, she didn't even have the means to dress herself decently. "I wish I could help. I'd like to see you in your own shop."

Abigail gave her a tight squeeze that filled Minerva with happiness. Then she disentangled herself from Minerva. "But you can. I'm going to make you look like a proper woman, Minerva. You're going to help me show people that there is more to me than Ebony White." She stood and held out her hand. "Please let me dress you."

Chapter Ten

A ren't you cold?"
Abigail giggled. She wasn't normally this giggly—but then again, she wasn't normally this happy. "How could I be cold when I'm around you?" she teased, mostly just to watch the high blush on Minerva's sharp cheekbones. "Raise your arms, please."

Minerva frowned at her, the kind of frown that probably put the fear of God into her students but only made Abigail giggle harder. "It's not that warm in here and you're not wearing anything." She sighed, a sound of satisfaction. "Not a single thing."

Abigail unrolled the corset she had sewn and wrapped it around Minerva's chest. "If it makes you uncomfortable, I can put my dress back on."

She hooked the busks together underneath Minerva's breasts and then began to tighten the laces. Through the thin—but not see-through—fabric of the new shift that Abigail had helped Minerva into, she could feel the older woman's body heat. There was something about dressing her, so soon after what they'd shared...

That something only got stronger when Minerva asked in a shy voice, "But then, what if I want to take your dress off later?"

100

Abigail laughed again as the corset tightened, suddenly revealing a shape that had been completely hidden before. "That would be a shame, wouldn't it? Especially since I'm dressing you at this exact moment in time."

Minerva gave her a weak smile. Abigail shouldn't tease her. She didn't want to do anything that would make Minerva start second-guessing what they had done in bed together. Because the moment she started to do that, she would undoubtedly talk herself out of ever doing anything like that again and then where would Abigail be?

Miserable, that's where. Taking what little comfort she could from Opal and gritting her teeth through the rest of it until she could get her shop.

She tied off the laces, leaving Minerva plenty of room to breathe. The hideous corset that Abigail had removed earlier was so large that Minerva probably had no idea how a proper set of stays was supposed to feel on her body.

"I'll at least put my shift back on."

Minerva snorted. "As if that would make any difference."

Abigail shook out the shirt that she had sewn, eyeing Minerva's newly prominent bosom and hoping that she wouldn't have to let the seams out. "That silk is not cheap. We import it all the way from France. Arms up," she said again.

She probably should put her own clothing back on. But she was enjoying the way that Minerva's eyes stroked over her skin. She was used to people looking at her in all stages of dress and undress. Long ago, when she had still been Miss Catherine's companion, she helped wash the girl's hair and dry her off after a bath. They'd gone swimming in a small stream behind the Whithall house and lay in the grass to dry and it had all been perfectly natural.

Or at least, it was when she was around other women. It was only the men who made her feel like her body was something tawdry and cheap. Not so much the customers of the Jeweled Ladies—because she was not cheap—but Mr. Dawson?

"Abigail," Minerva said softly. She stepped in closer and, after only a moment's hesitation, put her hands on Abigail's bare shoulders. "What is it?"

She tried to smile off. "Nothing. But I will dress if you want me to."

Minerva tilted her head to the side, then gently pressed her lips against Abigail's. The kiss didn't pack the same kind of heat that had effortlessly flowed between them earlier, but its sweetness was almost as arousing. "I want you to do what you want."

It was ridiculous, the way the back of her throat tightened and her eyes pricked. She laughed again until the feelings went away. "I want people to see you the way I see you."

Minerva looked at the shirt Abigail was still holding. At the rate they were going, that was going to take all night and perhaps the better part of the morning. "I don't understand how you see me. I am exactly what I am—an old spinster who is going to spend the rest of her life teaching children how to read in a one-room schoolhouse."

Abigail slid the shirt over her head. "Is that how you see yourself? An old spinster?" Even though she knew Minerva could button her own shirt, she did it anyway.

The shirt fit perfectly, highlighting Minerva's bosom and tapering down to her newly slender waist. "This is far too tight," Minerva protested.

"Move your arms. If it pulls, I can let it out. But," she added, winking at Minerva, "it won't pull."

Minerva rotated her arms and swung them back and forth. The shirt moved with her. It didn't pull across the shoulders one bit.

"See?"

"It's far too tight to be decent," Minerva grumbled.

"That's why there's a jacket. A perfectly respectable navy."

Minerva tried a different line of attack. "I thought you were going to sew me a dress?"

"You'll get more use out of a shirt and skirt. Trust me." She took the matching skirt out of the basket. "And you can take the jacket off when it gets warmer. You'll like it, I promise."

Minerva looked down at her newly lifted bosom. "This isn't decent, I tell you. I'm twenty-eight years old. I've never been married. In fact, you're only the second person I've ever kissed. And the first time, it didn't go very well."

"Twenty-eight is not old. Here, step into the skirt."

Minerva did so, balancing herself on Abigail's shoulders. "How old are you?"

Abigail focused on the skirt for a few moments while she tried to pick up the right answer. But there was no right answer and she didn't want to fight this kind of truth. "I don't know. I told Mistress I was twenty, but that was almost two years ago. I think I'm nineteen or twenty."

She hazarded a glance at Minerva's face and then quickly looked away. She didn't want to see that kind of pity. She was done being pitied. "Mrs. Whithall said I was the same age as Miss Catherine, but we didn't think so. I was always a year or two ahead of her. I developed before she did and I got my courses before she did and it just didn't seem like we were both eleven when it happened. I always felt older."

"You loved her."

Abigail nodded and swiped her hand across her eyes. "She even asked her mother if I could learn to read once. And Mrs. Whithall treated me kindly. A lot of people didn't get what I had. I had a good friend and a roof over my head and food to eat. Mrs. Whithall hardly ever hit me. It wasn't bad. But I wasn't free and then…"

Minerva's arms were around her, pulling her in and resting her head against her bosom. "Are you sure you don't wish to tell me?"

No one else knew about this. No one except Mistress, that was. And she only knew because she had come for Abigail. She would never know why Mistress had chosen to save her when there were so many other women in the same situation or even worse.

She didn't talk about the past of the Jeweled Ladies. None of them did. There, you were the closest of friends with someone if you told them your real name. Despite the fact that she'd had sex countless times with Opal, she didn't know the girl's name.

Emmy—Emerald Green—had been kind to her before she'd been accepted by the other girls. Sadie—Sapphire Bleu—was the only one who Abigail had come close to telling about the horrors she'd survived because Sadie understood whips and chains, in her own way. But even then, Abigail hadn't been able to bring herself to put it into words.

Nonoci would understand—but her wounds were too fresh. Abigail couldn't bring more pain into that girl's life. All she could do was offer her the support she needed.

Pasts and futures didn't exist at the Jeweled Ladies. There was only the now. It was better that way. Because if she didn't talk about it, she didn't have to think about it. Forgetting was a luxury she had now.

"What happened isn't important," she said, pushing out of Minerva's soft arms. Then she waited. Would Minerva push the issue again? Or would she let it drop?

She let it drop. Mostly. "It *is* important because it happened to you. But we don't have much time tonight, do we?"

"No," Abigail said with far more relief than she'd expected to feel. "I have to be gone before sunrise. Let me pin up the hem for you."

They were silent as Abigail worked. When she had the hem adjusted, she sat back and looked Minerva up and down. Really, the right clothes made all the difference in the world.

Gone was the frumpy, harsh spinster and in her place was a woman who was quite lovely. Minerva Krenshaw had a trim, youthful figure. Without her glasses, her eyes were a wide, clear brown. She looked less pinched and Abigail was fascinated by the smile that lurked in the corners of her mouth.

She got to her feet and circled Minerva. She needed to take in the waist of the skirt another inch—but would Minerva let her? Or would that be too scandalous? Either way, it was still a considerably better fit than that terrible dress she had been wearing. "This is how I see you, my dear. You're not some ancient, dried-up hunk of meat."

Minerva stared down at her front, smoothing her hands over the new skirt. "It is remarkably soft..." she admitted.

"How does the corset feel? It'll take a little while to break in but then it'll mold to your body and you'll feel much better in it. It won't rub, I promise," she said as she made it back to Minerva's front. "It's not a sin to be comfortable, you know."

Minerva's gaze travelled up Abigail's naked body. The raw longing in her gaze made Abigail's nipples tighten and her body grow heavy with desire.

And then Minerva's eyes shuttered. It was as if someone had blown a candle out, throwing the room into darkness. "But what we did, it *is* a sin."

She shrugged. "I like you. You like me. Maybe that is a sin but how could it be the same as..." Unexpectedly, her eyes started watering.

Minerva covered her mouth and took a step forward. "As what was done to you?"

Abigail nodded. Where was this emotion coming from? It wasn't wanted and wasn't necessary. Normally, it was easy to hide this away.

But this wasn't just some random customer. This was Minerva and she cared. At least, Abigail hoped she cared, anyway. She took a couple of deep breaths and tried to refocus on something else. Like the fact that Minerva looked both proper and gorgeous in her new clothes.

"I'll never be a proper woman," she said, trying to smile through the ache in the pit of her stomach.

Minerva might give in to her desire and her curiosity once—but really, was the woman capable of anything more than that? Or would she spend the next week, month, year—the next lifetime—punishing herself for what she thought of as her sins?

"But you'll get your shop. You can go somewhere where no one knows about your..." Her what? Minerva didn't finish the sentence.

It hurt to think that all she would ever be to this woman was a sin waiting to happen. God, she was so tired of being boiled down to one or two things—her color or her pussy—and treated as if the rest of her wasn't important.

"I'll always be a colored girl, a former slave, a former whore." Minerva flinched at the word, but Abigail didn't stop, didn't try to soften the words. This was her truth and she would not protect Minerva from it.

She wanted more from Minerva but if the woman couldn't give it to her, then it was better to know that now and only have her heart broken a little bit. "I'll never be free of that, no matter what I do. You worry about doing something wrong and being damned to hell—well, I've been there and it was never something *I* did. It was always something someone else decided for me because I wasn't free. Even whoring myself—what choice did I have? I was ruined anyway and not because I fell in love and gave myself away. Every sin I've supposedly committed was a sin committed against me. I made a promise a long time ago that I was going to live and that's what I'm going to do. I'll do what I have to in order to get the life I want, not the life someone else thinks I deserve. I suffered enough. I've got nothing to hide."

Literally. She was still completely nude.

Minerva looked like someone had slapped her and Abigail wished that this was a softer truth. For all of her hardness, Minerva was still such an innocent sometimes. So she went on in a gentle voice, "All your talk of sin, Minerva—and all I want to do is love you. Even a little bit, if you'll let me. Because I know that love is good and strong and God gave us these feelings for a reason. I know love is why I'm still alive."

Her voice caught as old, well-loved memories of playing dolls and sewing dresses with Miss Catherine tried to bubble up. She had loved Miss Catherine. If only...

A tear spilled down Minerva's cheek, calling Abigail back to herself. She couldn't save Miss Catherine now. All she could do was honor her promise to the girl. She would live, damn it all. "My shop—it'll keep me fed and safe and clothed. Those are all things I need to live. But you know what? No matter how successful that shop is, no matter how much I put into it, it won't love me back. It won't wrap its arms around me in the dead of night when I have a bad dream and tell me it'll be all right. It won't kiss me awake in the morning. It'll never look at me as if it'd die without me. That shop will never love me back and if loving you, even just a little bit for a little while, is a sin, then *so be it*."

For the longest moment, nothing happened. Minerva stood there, still as a stone, looking horrified.

Abigail turned away, unable to bear the thought of seeing rejection in Minerva's eyes. She scooped her shift up off the floor. "No matter what," she said, trying not to cry, "this is between us. I won't tell anyone."

Minerva's hands came down on her shoulders. "Wait."

Abigail paused, but she didn't turn around. She couldn't.

Or so she thought—until Minerva moved. Slowly, she began to trace a single fingertip over the scars haphazardly scoring Abigail's back. Abigail stiffened. Normally, no one saw the scars. Or, if they did, they ignored the violence the marks told tales of. Abigail worked on her back. Men looking for a fuck didn't want to think about that kind of violence and if they did, they went to Sadie instead.

"You talk of love," Minerva said in a voice that bordered on terrified. Abigail had to close her eyes against that terror. She had to. Minerva's finger kept tracing her history on her back. "Of wanting someone, of being with them. I've spent years convincing myself that I don't need any of that. More, that I don't want it. I never wanted it."

"But you do," she whispered.

Minerva's hand came flat on her back, warm and soft. The scars felt different under Minerva's touch. The skin was twisted and lumpy. Some of the cuts had gotten infected so the scars were even worse.

"I look at you—all of you—and..." Minerva's breath was a sigh against her ear. "And you make me face the fact that it was a lie. Everything I told myself—it was a lie. Because I was afraid."

109

"Minerva—"

"I don't want to be afraid anymore," she interrupted, her voice the barest of whispers. "You're the bravest woman I've ever met and I want to be stronger for you. You deserve happiness, my darling girl. I just wish…I wish I could give it to you."

Abigail turned, pulling her into her arms. They fit so nicely. Minerva was a little taller than she was, so it just made sense that Abigail tucked her head against her shoulder and nuzzled into her neck.

They just made sense together.

"What do we do now?"

"We continue on. No one else knows about our lessons, so we keep meeting. I don't have to work on Sundays so I can come see you. As long as I'm gone before sunrise, we should be safe. No one will know."

She could feel Minerva's lips move against her forehead—a smile? But then her body stiffened. "Wait—Mistress knows." She started to pull away. "Does she know…*everything*?"

Abigail clutched at Minerva's waist to keep her close. "I haven't told her anything other than you're teaching me to read. But she suspects, I'm sure."

Minerva was breathing harder now and the sight of her panic filled Abigail with dread. "Minerva," she said in a calm voice, like she was talking to a scared kitten. "Mistress would never say anything, one way or the other."

"But she knows!" Minerva lurched away from her. She shivered. "She…she caught me staring. At you. In the dry-goods store the day you were getting fabrics for that Native girl. *She knows*," she repeated miserably.

Now it was Abigail's turn to step in close, to put her hands on Minerva's shoulders. "She probably does. But," she added quickly before Minerva could start wailing, "her entire livelihood is based on keeping this town's secrets. If she started telling what she knows about the people in this town, they'd run her out before daybreak. No, they'd tar and feather her. They'd *ruin* her. The reason they haven't is because she keeps their secrets. And ours." She pressed a kiss to Minerva's shoulder. "I promise. She won't say a thing."

Minerva dropped her head into her hands. "Good God, how am I supposed to face my pupils tomorrow, after what we did in this room tonight?"

"The same way you've faced them every day for the last ten years. The same way I face the gentlemen every night." She stepped away and grabbed the matching jacket. She slid it over Minerva's arms and settled it on her shoulders. "How long have you known that you wanted to kiss a girl?"

"Years," Minerva said in a small voice.

"Before your first kiss?"

Minerva nodded.

"And yet," Abigail went on, turning Minerva so she could button the jacket and check the fit, "you did not tell anyone. Instead, you hid behind awful dresses and those glasses and you refused all attentions from any interested gentlemen?"

Minerva nodded again, and then she took a fortifying breath.

"Don't be afraid. They can't see what goes on here," she told the woman, placing her hand over Minerva's heart. "They never could."

111

"I…" Minerva sighed heavily and covered Abigail's hand with hers. "We'll meet tomorrow in the church for our regular lesson?"

That was as good as she was going to get right now, she knew. To push Minerva for anything more would send her spinning off into panic. "I'll bring the tea. Will you be there at four?"

It wasn't confident or seductive, that smile. It barely even qualified as a smile at all. But when Minerva said, "I might be a little early," relief coursed through Abigail.

She would try, this prim schoolteacher. She was willing to try this romance, no matter how sinful and improper and wrong it might be to love a woman such as Abigail.

"I might be early, too."

Chapter Eleven

The whole day, Minerva struggled. She felt too large for her skin, afraid that she might burst from the pressure to turn inside out all over again.

She couldn't look at her desk without flushing because that was where Abigail had first made her come apart. She couldn't even go back and hide in her room because the smell of Abigail still lingered on the bedding.

Everywhere Minerva looked, something reminded her of Abigail.

This was why she had left New York. She couldn't bear to be around Eliza and see her sin reflected back at her.

She would not leave Brimstone. Perhaps she could be forgiven in the eyes of the Lord for being swept away once. But to stay was to make a choice. To stay and continue to see Abigail would be to choose, of her own volition, to continue the torrid affair—if that's what this was. It felt like an affair, illicit and all-encompassing.

It was like she told her students. Fool me once, shame on you. Fool me twice, shame on me.

How big a fool was she?

She climbed the stairs in the Methodist Church,

fully aware that she was about to make a fool of herself all over again and equally aware of the fact that she simply could not help herself.

It was as plain as the nose on Minerva's face that the girl had not had an easy life, no matter how much she'd cared for her Miss Catherine. The man who'd trapped her in a web of lies, whoever he was, had sinned against Abigail. She wasn't any different from any of the men and women who had made that stop in her parents' kitchen, risking everything for a chance at freedom and happiness.

Slavery was illegal. But the scars still lasted. Maybe they always would—Abigail's back would never magically heal.

But Abigail didn't let that stop her. That girl was willing to risk everything for Minerva, for a little love and sweetness. For a kind of freedom that Minerva hadn't even known existed.

Who was Minerva to refuse her? To judge Abigail and declare her a sinner? They were all born into sin anyway.

Though it would still be better if they weren't in the Methodist Church.

All of these thoughts rattled around Minerva's head as she gained the balcony in the church. She had come directly from the schoolroom. It probably wasn't even three twenty. She had been half hopeful and half afraid that Abigail would already be here.

She did not wait long.

"Good afternoon," Abigail said in a voice that was practically demure. She all but floated over to where Minerva was perched on her pew. Abigail bent and pressed a quick kiss to Minerva's lips. But before she could react, Abigail straightened and cast a critical eye over her dress. "At least tell me you're wearing the corset?"

It was so tempting to defend her Sunday dress. It had been her best one, after all. "I am. But I do not think I got it as tight as you did."

Abigail wrinkled her brow. "I don't suppose I can convince you to burn that dress, can I?"

"I'll have you know this is a perfectly respectable dress," she bristled.

Abigail set down the basket she carried and then pulled out the skirt. "I fixed the hem. Would you at least let me alter that dress? On Sunday?"

That was what she said. What she meant was, *can I come back on Sunday and lie with you again?*

If she were a decent woman, Minerva would say no. But perhaps she was not as decent as she had thought. "Will you promise not to stop and ask directions?"

With a laugh, Abigail sat down on the pew, right next to Minerva. She wrapped her arms around Minerva's waist and tucked her head against her shoulder and squeezed her. Without thinking, Minerva's arms came around her and she tilted Abigail's head back so that she could see her face underneath the brim of her fancy hat. "I'll do my best," Abigail murmured.

And then Minerva was kissing her and for the first time all day, she just felt right because she was kissing Abigail and in that moment, she knew. This was her choice. She *chose* Abigail.

However, they were still in the house of God. She broke away from the kiss. "I'm supposed to be teaching you." It was her last grasp at sanity.

115

"Oh, I don't know. That seemed fairly educational to me," Abigail replied with a smile as she removed her fine hat. But Minerva was happy to see that the color in her cheeks had deepened and she was breathing hard.

Somehow, it was reassuring to see that Abigail, with her vast experience, was just as affected as Minerva was. "Lessons first," she said crisply. But she didn't let go of Abigail. She found she couldn't.

So she didn't. The entire lesson, they sat together like that, Minerva's arm around Abigail's shoulder. Every time Abigail read a word correctly, Minerva would kiss her.

It didn't take long before the kisses got longer than the lessons. The reading lessons, anyway. Minerva was trying admirably to study how Abigail touched her mouth, where it felt best, where Minerva didn't feel much of anything at all. This was merely a subject upon which she was expanding her knowledge. There would be no homework and there would be no test on the matter. There would only be a continued study.

All of that was well and good except that she was kissing Abigail and Abigail was kissing her back and every time their mouths met, Minerva's skin got tighter and the heavy weight between her legs got heavier and all she wanted to do was run her fingers over that secret spot of Abigail's and...

She wanted to taste Abigail—but wasn't she already doing that with each kiss? She wanted to touch her, to feel her again. She wanted *more*.

Last time, she'd accidentally slipped her fingers inside of Abigail's body. She hadn't seen what she was doing, only felt the wet warmth of the girl's body

116

as it gave under her awkward attentions. Suddenly, Abigail's heat, tight and tempting, had surrounded her fingers. The shock of it had been so intense that she wasn't sure she remembered it rightly.

She wanted to plunge her fingers into Abigail's body again and again, this time, sitting back on her heels and watching as Abigail took her inside. She wanted to watch Abigail's fingers disappear into her body. She wanted to understand why she wanted these things in a logical, empirical way.

A noise somewhere outside the church broke into their silent worship. Minerva jolted back to herself, breathing so hard that she was lightheaded. Is this how it was going to be? Now that she had decided to give herself over to this temptation, she wouldn't be able to *not* give herself over to it?

What time was it? Were people coming into the church? Dear God. She needed to go. She looked down at Abigail, her dark lashes standing out against the pale brown of her cheeks, at the little curve to the corners of her lips swollen with Minerva's kisses and all she wanted to do was ignore the world outside and go back to the lessons in kissing. Her thirst for knowledge was *vast*. She could spend a lifetime learning this girl.

Abigail straightened and reached for her hat. Minerva took an odd sort of pride in that she had not mussed up the girl's hair. "Will I see you tomorrow?" she asked like a besotted, lovesick fool. Because she already knew the answer—no. They were risking so much meeting in this church and that was under the guise of a legitimate educational enterprise. Anything else would be foolhardy to the point of suicidal.

At least Abigail looked resigned about it as she said, "I don't think so. But we have another lesson on Wednesday?" Minerva nodded eagerly. "Will do me a favor?"

"Of course, dear girl."

Abigail looked pleased at that. Her eyelashes fluttered and the color of her cheeks deepened. "Will you wear your new shirt and jacket on Wednesday?"

All of the good feelings that had been bouncing around inside of Minerva ran headlong into each other, creating a sickening crunch that she swore she could hear. Maybe that was just whatever was happening outside. "People might notice the change."

Abigail laughed, light and carefree. It was the kind of sound that Minerva could get drunk on—but she didn't drink. Just one more thing that she didn't know anything about that Abigail probably did.

"Minerva, that's the point. But it's a change for the better, I promise you. You'll see. And that way I can make any final adjustments."

Minerva nodded, trying to find a logical reason for the pit in her stomach and coming up empty. After all, Abigail had gone to a great deal of trouble to make her new clothes. The least she could do was actually wear the things. "All right. I will."

Abigail's face lit up with the kind of smile that simply took Minerva's breath away and then the girl leaned down and kissed her until all Minerva could think about was making Abigail smile again.

All it would take would be wearing some fine clothes.

How hard could it be?

*

"What has you looking so happy?"

Abigail looked up from where she knelt in front of Mrs. Logan in the Dupree parlor. "Do I look happy?"

Mrs. Emmeline Dupree notched a knowing eyebrow at Abigail as Mrs. Logan harrumphed. "You are smiling," the older woman said without moving.

Abigail thought quickly. Emmy was a friend but that didn't mean that Abigail wanted to share her new happiness with her. And Mrs. Logan was a customer only—and an unwilling one at that. "I'm just thrilled that you're giving me the chance to make you a dress, Mrs. Logan."

Mrs. Logan scowled, but Abigail thought she saw a hint of a smile before she turned her attention back to the hem of the dress. "I do not see why you've decided I must have a new dress, Mrs. Dupree."

"Because," Emmy said smoothly. "You need one and Miss White needs to sew you one. Everyone wins."

"I am also sewing one for Miss Krenshaw," Abigail said before she realized the words were out there. Oh, heavens. At least she hadn't said Minerva, but honestly.

"Is that so?" Emmy leaned forward, studying Abigail closely and Abigail remembered that, before she'd fallen in love with the mayor of Brimstone, Emmy had been Mistress's chosen successor. "How interesting."

"She's teaching me to read," Abigail offered weakly. Her only hope was diverting the women's attentions away from her dressing Minerva.

119

"She is?" Emmy said it in such a tone that Abigail looked up sharply, a pin flying from her mouth.

"Mistress arranged it."

"Why, that's wonderful." Emmy smiled warmly, but Abigail thought there was something else in her eyes, something surprised.

And again, Abigail had to wonder why no one at the Jeweled Ladies had bothered to teach her. There was lots of time when they weren't working. The girls chatted and read and knit and Abigail sewed.

Why hadn't anyone—especially Emmy, who Abigail called a friend—taught her her letters?

"It is going to be very pretty," Mrs. Logan said, looking down wistfully.

Abigail smiled. Even Mrs. Logan—who was not a warm person—got excited about a new dress. "And perfectly proper," Abigail reminded her. "Between Mrs. Dupree, you and Miss Krenshaw, this town will see that I can sew dresses for respectable ladies."

"Hmph." That was Mrs. Logan's favorite noise to make. Abigail hadn't yet figured out if it was a noise of disapproval or not.

"Just the other day, I caught Cynthia Hobbs eyeing my dress," Emmy said over the rim of her tea cup.

Hope flared in Abigail's chest. Cynthia Hobbs was the banker's daughter and usually quite turned out. She bought at least one new dress every season. "Did she ask where you had it made?"

Emmy laughed and Mrs. Logan snorted again. "Oh, no—she gave me the cut, as usual. But that doesn't stop her father from doing business with me or her from wanting the finest dresses in town."

"Not that anyone would accuse me of being the best dressed woman in this town," Mrs. Logan muttered.

Abigail repressed a smile. "The dress doesn't make the woman—the woman makes the dress." If only she could help Minerva see that.

"We should have a plan." Emmy got up and looked at Mrs. Logan. Once, every dress Abigail had sewn for the former Jewel had been a vivid emerald green to match her name. But now Emmy wore soft blues and deep golds that made her seem a different woman. "Something that announces to the town that you are responsible for the best dresses."

"We can't just declare that I sewed the dress." Abigail knew that her word alone wouldn't be enough for Cynthia Hobbs.

"It would be best if someone asked in a crowd," Mrs. Logan said. "An innocent exchange. Saturday at the dry-goods store, perhaps. It's always busy then."

All three women fell silent as they pondered this suggestion. Would Minerva be able to do that? Stand in front of a large group and discuss what she was wearing? Heavens, she could barely think of wearing the dresses in public without dying of fright. Mrs. Logan, however, would have no problem announcing the origins of her newest dress to the world at large. As far as Abigail could tell, the older woman feared nothing—especially not public censure.

"I'm sure that Mrs. Synder would be happy to help," Emmy said slowly.

"For a price," Mrs. Logan agreed. "That woman would sell her first born if the offer was high enough."

"I will have to see if Miss Krenshaw would be

comfortable doing that," Abigail hedged as she finished the hem. She climbed to her feet. "I'm still working on her dress so it would be several weeks before we could arrange that."

Emmy clapped her hands. "This will work. I'll take care of arranging it and you just focus on sewing." She laid a hand on Abigail's shoulder. "We'll get you that shop, Abigail. Now that you're learning to read, you're almost there. I do so want to see you happy."

A few months ago, Abigail would've forced a smile and a lie to her lips—she was perfectly happy where she was. But now? After falling into Minerva's bed?

She wanted more than just her shop to sustain her. She wanted love.

She wanted Minerva.

"So do I," she admitted as Emmy pulled her into a hug. For so long, happiness had seemed out of reach, something unnecessary to survival.

Minerva had shown her otherwise and now Abigail dared to hope she could have it all.

*

As she climbed the stairs to the balcony of the Methodist Church for the second time that week, Abigail held her breath. Which Minerva would be waiting for her?

It took a moment for her eyes to adjust to the dim light but when they did, she saw that Minerva was not sitting in her normal spot in the pew by the window. Instead, she was standing, her back to the stairs.

Abigail could see through the fabric of the new jacket that her shoulders were tight.

She'd worn the new clothes. That realization brought a smile to Abigail's lips. But it was quickly followed by a second thought—Minerva was not comfortable in them.

Still, she was trying and that was hopeful. "How did it go?" Abigail asked, hoping for the best and bracing for anything but.

She saw Minerva take a deep breath before she turned around. If anything, the woman's expression was twice as pinched as normal. No, she was not comfortable at all.

"Fine," she said briskly. If Abigail didn't know any better, she might have thought that Minerva was being her normal prickly self.

But she knew better. "Oh?" she asked, moving closer.

Minerva didn't say anything else until Abigail had set down the picnic basket, removed her hat and then stepped to Minerva, wrapping the stiff woman in her arms. "It was fine," she repeated. Her voice shook a little. "I'm just not used to having people notice me, that's all."

Abigail kissed her on the forehead. "Like how?"

Long moments passed. Abigail let her hands stroke over Minerva's back, willing her to be calm. "You must think me silly. What woman doesn't want compliments?" This last part came out almost as a wail, the sound of pure misery.

But even as she was miserable with Minerva, she was also hopeful. People had noticed the new outfit. Not only that, they'd complimented Minerva on it.

"It's not silly. You're just not used to it, that's all. Do you want to tell me what happened?" Like, who'd noticed? Were they women who needed dresses? What had Minerva said?

Minerva shrugged, another hedge against the truth. "Some of the students, the girls—they said I looked very pretty in my new dress. And then, walking here, it seemed like...like people—well, that people noticed me more. They wished me a good afternoon and remarked upon the lovely weather. They *talked* to me, Abigail." She said that as if she'd been offered money for flipping up her new skirt.

She leaned back. "Are you saying that people don't normally talk to you?"

Minerva nodded. "Why would they? I'm the schoolteacher. I'm sour and I don't hold my tongue. It's not a bad thing," she added quickly as Abigail stared at her. "There's a certain measure of freedom with being invisible in the crowd and..." She took a deep breath. "And I didn't have that today. But don't worry. I—I can adjust."

Abigail wasn't sure how much she believed that statement. After all, Minerva was currently in her arms, shaking.

"Here. Let me look at you. Were you very uncomfortable?" Abigail asked as Minerva stood there, her arms unnaturally tense at her side.

She tried to shrug. "The clothes are better than I thought they would be. I think they just take a little getting used to. They fit differently."

"Thank heavens for that," Abigail murmured, smoothing out the wool on Minerva's sleeves. If she had made this outfit for anyone else, she would've taken the fabric in another inch or two to highlight Minerva's figure. She may not feel natural in these clothes, but she was *made* to wear them.

But another inch or two might actually kill the woman and Abigail couldn't have that. "There's only one thing better than you in these clothes."

"Oh? What' s that?"

Abigail leaned up on her toes and brushed a kiss over Minerva's lips. Somehow, she had to wait until Sunday before she could be herself again. Until then, she would remain Ebony White. "You out of these clothes," she whispered against Minerva' s lips.

That sigh—the sound of Minerva letting go of her worries—that was a very good thing. That was the sound of pleasure, just waiting to be had. And Abigail was tired of waiting. So she kissed this woman, slipping her tongue into her mouth and tasting the tart sweetness that was Minerva.

"I think of you constantly," Minerva murmured some minutes later. "I can't think of anything *but* you."

"Do you?" There was very little of Minerva's skin showing—but her ears were exposed, as was the barest suggestion of her neck above the collar of the shirt. Abigail took full advantage of what she had to work with, pressing kisses on Minerva's jaw and sucking her earlobe in between her teeth. "Have you touched yourself yet, my darling woman?"

"*What?*" she asked in a shuddering voice. But then again, everything was shuddering as Abigail nipped at the small inch of skin right below her ear.

"When we were together on Sunday, you said you had never explored yourself. Have you, now that you know what is waiting for you on the other side?"

Minerva made a sort of squeaking noise, as if Abigail had just said the most scandalous thing ever.

Well, maybe she had. After all, this was Miss Minerva Krenshaw. No one else would dare say such things to her.

Abigail dared. "Tonight," she whispered close to Minerva's ear, "when you lay on the bed, think of me and how you want to touch me on Sunday. Slide your hands between your legs and think of me." Abigail pressed her knee between Minerva's legs. It wasn't a lot—there were several skirts in between her leg and Minerva's little button of pleasure, but Minerva whimpered all the same.

"Consider this your assignment," Abigail murmured, rolling her thumb over that tight bud and kissing her way to the other ear. "I want you to touch yourself when you're all alone in that bed, thinking of me. You don't have to shatter," she added, knowing that would be asking a lot of the woman. "You just have to think about what you're feeling. And I am coming to you on Sunday, Minerva. Wild horses could not keep me away."

"They couldn't?" she asked and in that question, Abigail heard a lifetime of being invisible—of being alone.

"No," she reassured her. "And when I get there, I'm going to take you to bed and kiss every inch of your body and stroke your pussy and suck your tits until…"

Minerva sagged against her knee, wedged between the skirts. "Until?"

"Until you scream. Until I'm yours and you are *mine*." She kissed Minerva with everything she had.

She'd never had a lover on her terms, just for herself. Owners, yes. Rapists, yes. Customers, yes.

None of those people had been for *her*. None of them had ever cared for her, for her pleasure, for her needs. And although Mistress had insisted that Abigail deserved those things…

She wasn't sure she'd been capable of them, capable of pleasure, capable of feeling power in a bed, over another person. She'd never wanted to dominate and control someone as she had been controlled, but she'd wondered for so long if she could make someone weak with want for *her*. For Abigail Whithall.

And she could.

Minerva moaned into her mouth. "I already am."

And with that, the lessons were forgotten.

The reading lessons, anyway.

Chapter Twelve

Touch *herself?*
        Touch herself?

That was what Abigail had said to do. But that night, as Minerva lay on her narrow, uncomfortable bed, she wasn't sure she knew how.

It wasn't as if she had never touched herself before. She had. She washed regularly. She kept herself clean.

But that had never... Well. She had *never* because that had *never*.

Until Abigail had touched her. She had walked Minerva backwards until she had been sitting on the desk and then she stepped between Minerva's legs and slid her hands over that most secret place. So secret, in fact, that Minerva had had no idea that pleasure could be found there.

How on earth was she supposed to find it herself? It didn't seem possible. But then again, she had touched Abigail right here, in this very bed, and the girl had seemed to enjoy it. Surely she wouldn't lie to protect Minerva's feelings, would she?

Now that she thought about it, Minerva wasn't sure she had ever touched herself without some unpleasant barrier. The cloth she used for bathing was rough. The soap was lye. There was nothing soft or gentle about her ablutions.

But here on this bed, everything had been different. Instead of water that was barely heated above cold, the bed with Abigail in it had been warm and inviting. Even just thinking about the way Abigail had, with a few touches and whispered words, driven her nearly to the point of insanity—all of it made her feel liquid and hot and heavy.

Her heart beating wildly, Minerva ran her fingers down the front of her nightgown. Nothing. Not a shiver of excitement nor a spark of heat. Just the same old body that she had been taking care of for her twenty-eight years.

She refused to be discouraged. After all, Abigail had said that she didn't have to shatter under her own hand. So, dutifully, she moved her hands lower. Small circular movements of the hand worked best, she was fairly sure. This was all just an…experiment. That was all. At least, that's what she tried to tell herself. Sometimes experiments gave you the results you desired and sometimes they didn't.

As she fumbled around under the sheets and the threadbare blanket, she began to wonder if this was an experiment that would give her no results at all.

She wished Abigail were here. Abigail would know what she was doing wrong and would show her the correct way to do this. She would climb under the covers with Minerva or kick them off entirely. They wouldn't miss them because Abigail was warmth and light and heat all at once. There would be nothing between them.

At that thought, Minerva lifted her hips and

129

dragged her nightdress up over them. Then she put her hand back between her legs and focused on the sensations.

The hair that covered her private places was soft and springy under her fingers. Her fingers moved lower, dipping into the cleft of skin hidden there. She'd never studied this area—empirically, that was. She had just done her business as quickly as she could. But it wasn't all one smooth expanse of flesh. She didn't know if she looked like Abigail. There was a tiny little bump that tightened when her fingers passed over it.

Further down was the place where she was reasonably sure her fingers had slipped inside of Abigail. Further down was where Abigail had rolled her onto her back and thrust her fingers up into her.

That was where Minerva bled from. She understood enough of basic human anatomy to know that that was where babies were born from and, if she were ever going to marry—which she would not—she was fairly certain that that was where her husband would claim her body. She thought.

She moved back to that little bump, the one that had responded to her touch. How had she made it this far in life without realizing it was there? She moved her fingers around in little circles, pinpointing exactly where the sensations spiked and when they fell off.

This was nothing compared to the way Abigail had made her feel. But there was still something there, something that intensified when she let her mind turned back to her mouth on Abigail's breasts, feeling those wide, dark nipples pucker and fit themselves to her mouth like they were made just for her.

130

Her body tightened and relaxed almost instantly, a pale ghost of pleasure compared to what she had experienced with Abigail. But it wasn't *nothing*. It was most definitely *something*. She lay there, breathing deeply as her mind began to drift in the state of relaxation. Tomorrow, she would see Abigail again. She would kiss her again—although they really must focus on the lessons. In the church, they must focus on reading. And then it would only be another three days until Sunday. It was wrong to sin so greatly on the day of the Lord, but it was the only day they had and Minerva couldn't help herself.

She drifted off, Abigail's back floated before her mind's eye. The scars had marred her otherwise perfect skin, made even worse in the dim light and deep shadows from her stove. That poor girl had suffered so greatly. Minerva was gripped by an overwhelming urge to protect her, to make sure that she was never again at someone's mercy. Her last conscious thought was that she would tell Abigail that on Sunday.

*

The minutes that ticked by until Sunday were interminable and Minerva counted each and every one of them. The sun acted as if it would never sink below the horizon. She had restricted herself to only making her bed twice this time, which she felt was progress. Once again, the schoolhouse was spotless. She had been somewhat negligent of her regular duties as she left earlier and earlier to meet Abigail at the church. The school had needed a good scrubbing.

Finally, the knock came on the front door. Minerva hurried to it and opened it cautiously, trying not to look too anxious just in case it was someone besides Abigail.

But of course, it wasn't. She was in her borrowed rags again and this time she had added the bent stick as a sort of cane to her outfit. Minerva allowed herself to exhale with relief as she stood aside and Abigail rather convincingly hobbled into the room. They were silent until Minerva had closed the door and thrown the bolt again.

"Did you see anyone this time?" she asked as Abigail began to remove the many layers.

"No, I came a different way. I didn't want to risk running into the Snyders again. That's why it took me so long to get here." She was back in that pale peach colored gown, safely hidden underneath the dull, drab dresses. "Come here," she said in a voice that was too tender by half as she held out her arms to Minerva.

And that was all they said for some time. They left a trail of clothing from the front door of the schoolhouse back to the bedroom. There was no stopping in front of the fire, no tentative kisses and hesitations. There was just Minerva's body and Abigail's and the many ways that they could come together.

"I didn't get the chance to ask," Abigail whispered as she rolled Minerva onto her back and began kissing down her neck to her breasts. "Did you touch yourself like I asked?"

"I... I did."

"Hmmm." She licked along Minerva's nipple and then proceeded to blow air over the tip.

132

Minerva's back arched as she clutched at Abigail's shoulders. "It didn't feel like that at all, when I touched myself there."

"Here?" Abigail ran the smooth fingernail around the tight bud of Minerva's nipple.

"Yes. But... Not like that."

And then Abigail's heat was away from her and she sat back on her heels between Minerva's legs. Her hands ran up and down Minerva's thighs, and there was a certain wickedness to be on view like this. "Show me."

Minerva recognized that tone of voice. It was one that she had used herself many, many times over the years in the classroom. The kind of voice that prompted the hesitant student out of his or her seat and to the front of the room to recite a poem or historical date that Minerva had informed them they must know by heart.

She smiled at the tone, at the warm familiarity of it, even though she was now the reluctant student.

Well, perhaps not *that* reluctant.

She skimmed her hands over her breasts and it did feel different today. But was that because she was naked, performing this action for Abigail's pleasure?

Abigail shook her head and laughed a little. "You are entirely too innocent, my dear woman. And I have to say, I rather like you like that."

"Why?" She didn't know what she was doing. She could never hope to match Abigail's knowledge and experience.

Even though the light in this room was dim—not as dim as before, because Minerva had carried a lamp back in so that she could better see what she wanted to touch and taste—despite that dimness, she could see something change in Abigail's eyes. "You're just for *me*. You don't realize how special that makes you."

Her hands moved up higher on Minerva's thighs, dipping along the insides and then sweeping back out. "I only want you," she told the girl because it was the truth and lying might be a sin, but the greater sin would be lying to Abigail. She didn't want any lies here, any falsehoods between them when there was nothing else. "No one but you."

Speaking those words aloud felt... Well, it felt perilously close to a vow.

Which was foolhardy at best because there could never be anything between them—nothing recognized by any church, Baptist, Catholic, Methodist, or any state in this Union. They were women and of different races. There would never be vows.

But there could still be a promise, couldn't there?

"When you touched yourself, did you find pleasure at all?" Minerva nodded. "Show me where. I want to see."

Heat flamed at her cheeks and raced down her chest, but Minerva did as she was told. It was all part of the experiment, after all.

Under Abigail's eye, she lifted her hand and tried to find the spot that had brought her a glimmer of relief a few days ago. "Here."

"And how did you touch herself there?" Abigail sounded calm and reasonable about this, but Minerva knew better. It was easier to watch Abigail than it was to watch what she was doing to herself and she saw that Abigail was breathing hard, her eyes darkening.

"Little circles." She demonstrated as best she

could. Although the motion was the same and she was in the same spot, everything else was different. "I don't understand why it's different."

Abigail continued to rub her hands up and down and over, inside and out of Minerva's thighs. "How do you mean?"

"Why didn't I ever feel this when I was in the bath?" Even having to ask the question was embarrassing but this was an educational experience and the only stupid question was one that never got asked.

Abigail's grin brightened the room. "What did you think of, when you were in the bath all those times you didn't feel anything?"

The pressure underneath that little bump of flesh was starting to build and Minerva's head couldn't stay still on the pillow. It was hard to think of anything but the pleasure and Abigail. "The water—it's always cold. I can never get it hot enough."

Abigail grimaced sympathetically. "I wish I could sneak you into the Jeweled Ladies, my darling. I would draw you a hot bath and then climb in with you and scrub you until you shined. And I would take the softest cloths and dry every inch of your body and braid your hair loosely around your head and lay you out on my bed and satisfy your every need before I took my pleasure of you."

Minerva cried out as these words settled over her, as sensual as a lover's kiss. Her hips bucked, but she didn't remove her hand. God, that sounded like…

Like home. Like something she wanted to do every night with this woman. Only with this woman.

"You see?" Abigail said, her voice thick with

need. "Do you see now why you can bring pleasure to yourself now but couldn't before?"

"No," she gasped as sensations rocketed through her. "I don't understand. Please, Abigail."

"It is because you think of me."

Then she leaned down and pushed Minerva's hand away from that secret, private place. But instead of replacing Minerva's fingers with her own, she did something eminently more scandalous.

She kissed Minerva, right there, right on that little bump hidden beneath the curls of hair tucked between Minerva's legs. Abigail pressed her lips to that secret spot and Minerva shattered. Well and truly shattered into a million tiny pieces and she knew that, no matter how much glue was involved, she would never be put back together again in exactly the same way.

And just when she thought she couldn't stand it for another moment, there was another sensation. Her eyes flew open and she looked down to see Abigail licking her. With her *tongue*. She had moved so that her fingers were holding the folds of Miranda's flesh apart and she was…she was…

A tiny part of her brain demanded Minerva put a stop to this. It was indecent and immoral and wrong in every possible way.

But that part was so small that it was easy to ignore. Minerva struggled to get air into her lungs as she sank her fingers into Abigail's hair, course and textured and yet still perfect because it was Abigail's hair, not anyone else's. She didn't push the girl's head away. Instead, like the shameless hussy she was becoming, she held Abigail to her and surrendered to the kisses.

Chapter Thirteen

A bigail had been wrong.

All of those times she had been with Opal, she'd thought that was what it was to pleasure a woman. She had never minded the taste of Opal, the perfumed smell of her. She had done this with Opal on several occasions, after all.

But in the moment that the sweet cream taste of Minerva filled her mouth and the earthy, tart smell of her filled Abigail's nose, she realized she was almost as unprepared for what was happening as Minerva so very obviously was.

Opal would giggle and arch her back and reach for the man who was paying them to do this to each other. She would delicately stroke Abigail's shoulders and brush her fingertips over Abigail's forehead as Abigail performed the task before her. It had all been playacting, every moment of it.

Everything about Minerva was real. The way her fingers found Abigail's hair and held her against her pussy—that wasn't faked. The way Minerva gasped and writhed so much that Abigail had to lock her arms around the woman's thighs and hold her still—that was real. And the way Minerva cried out her name and she shattered again, sending sharp spikes of need deep into Abigail's body—that wasn't a performance. Not from either of them.

Minerva's pussy—indeed, her entire body—shuddered and shook before going completely limp. Abigail lightened her touches, pressing little kisses against the lips of Minerva's pussy and that tiny nub of pleasure. She spread her kisses to her soft belly and the sweet skin on the inside of her thigh. She waited patiently until Minerva's breath slowed before she moved, covering Minerva's body with her own. Her nipples were hard as she dragged them over the planes of Minerva's stomach then up until their breasts were pressed together. Then she propped herself on her elbows and stared down at Minerva.

"Well?" she asked, shifting so that Minerva's thigh was between her legs and hers was between Minerva's legs. "Questions?"

Minerva laughed out loud. "In another life, you would have made an excellent teacher, my dear girl."

Abigail grinned at the compliment and then shifted her hips. Minerva lifted her thigh, pushing against Abigail's pussy. "I would've made a very poor teacher. I heard they had to be prim and proper."

Minerva laughed again. It was such a light, carefree sound—it took ten years off her. "They also have to dress poorly, I've heard. And it would be a shame to see you dressed poorly because you are so very beautiful." She cupped Abigail's face in her palms and, after only a moment's hesitation, kissed her full on the lips.

The kiss deepened as Abigail shifted her hips back and forth, letting her body push her down on Minerva's thigh. Slow, languorous heat built from that point of contact. She was in no hurry. They had hours until sunrise and she would not waste them. Not a single one.

She didn't know how long they lay there, kissing and touching and petting. Because Minerva was petting her. Her hands were stroking over Abigail's cheeks, down her back, upper arms. A few times, she got bold and cupped Abigail's bottom in her hands before retreating back up to her shoulders again. And through it all, Minerva kissed her mouth and her jaw and her neck.

It felt decadent, this slow, satisfying lovemaking. There was a clock ticking—she was pretty sure it was the watch fob that Minerva wore pinned to her breast every day. They could not stay here forever.

The minutes that passed were warm and soft and gentle. God, so gentle, so filled with care it almost made her want to cry.

And when Minerva whispered, "Oh, my dearest girl, my sweet Abigail," in her ear, Abigail realized something like a bolt out of the blue.

She didn't want to go back to the brothel. She didn't want to spend tomorrow night or the next night or the night after that or any night, ever, flat on her back, her skirts flipped up as another man shoved his rod into her. She didn't want to worry about getting a disease or getting pregnant with some stranger's baby anymore. She didn't want to be that person anymore.

She wanted to be *this* person, the person who spent her evenings in the privacy of this room with *this* woman.

"I don't know if I can kiss you like that," Minerva whispered against her neck. "But I want to touch you,

139

my sweet Abigail. I want to make you feel like you make me feel."

Abigail pushed up onto her elbows and stared down at Minerva. Her hair was spread out over the pillowcase and her eyes lidded with satisfaction. No one else got to see her like this. She prayed that no one else ever would. "You don't have to do anything you don't want. But I want you to touch me very badly."

But neither of them moved for a moment. Not until Minerva said, "Will you help me?"

"Always." And it was true.

She rolled onto her back and this time, instead of stretching out alongside her, Minerva lay on top of her. Abigail could see that she was trying to replicate the position they had just been in—which was a perfectly fine position. But it wouldn't be enough for her.

"I need you to touch me," she said after another deep kiss. "God, Minerva, I've never needed anything so much."

She needed to survive. She needed food and water and shelter and safety. She needed her freedom. But now that she had achieved all of those things? Now they weren't enough anymore. Now she needed something more than just survival.

She needed to live. She needed passion and hope and, yes, love.

God, she hoped she could have a little love.

She could sense the nervous hesitation even as the woman kissed her with raw, unbridled passion that made the whole thing sweeter. It was silly to think that somehow, Minerva made her feel more real. Abigail had never *not* been real. She'd always been a whole person, no matter what Mrs. Whithall or Mr. Dawson

140

thought. No matter what had been done to her, no one had ever been able to take away the fact that she was Abigail Whithall.

But for the first time, Abigail felt like she could choose who that person was—and that person was someone who was falling for Miss Minerva Krenshaw.

This new person whom she was becoming was someone who didn't wait for permission. She took what she wanted.

Like right now. She lifted Minerva's hand from where it was rubbing over her tight nipple and licked the tips of the woman's fingers. Then she guided Minerva's hand down until it was stroking at the top of her pussy. "Yes," she breathed, her head falling back onto the pillow. "Right there, darling."

She didn't let go of Minerva's hand. Together, they worked her body. Minerva's mouth came down on Abigail's breasts again, sucking and licking and—

"Oh, God," Abigail whispered as Minerva blew a stream of air over her nipple.

"Good?" But instead of that nervous tone, Minerva suddenly sounded confident.

Abigail's eyes flew open and she caught Minerva staring at her. That woman knew what she was doing to Abigail—she could see it in the knowing smile, the wicked gleam of her eyes.

"You're a very good student," was all Abigail could say because her body was suddenly beyond her control and there was a moment of panic because she'd spent years fighting for control over her emotions because that was all she *could* control.

But Minerva had her hands and mouth everywhere and she whispered, "My sweet Abigail, let

141

me take care of you," and Abigail was able to let go of that precious control and instead focus on the way Minerva's fingers were rubbing against the nub of her pleasure and her mouth was sucking down on Abigail's tit.

And then the warm wetness of Minerva's mouth was gone and the woman was shifting, climbing between Abigail's legs. "I want to see this time," she said in a voice husky with desire. "I didn't get to see when I did this last time."

"What?"

Abigail didn't get any further than that before Minerva, still rubbing that tight nub, slid her other hand over Abigail's pussy. "Is it—are you always this wet?" she asked, a mix of innocence and pure lust.

God, Abigail loved that pure lust on her. "No. You make me that wet."

Minerva paused and shifted Abigail's hips toward the dim light of the lamp. Then her hands were back on Abigail's body, rubbing and stroking and making Abigail wetter. "I want to be inside you," Minerva whispered, touching Abigail's pussy as if it were a holy thing. "*Here*. Is that wrong?"

"No," Abigail moaned, lifting one leg and wrapping her ankle around Minerva's hip. She began to stroke her own breasts, teasing the stiff points as she watched Minerva explore her.

"I just..." Her sexy confidence was gone, replaced by confusion again.

"One finger." She circled her pussy, her fingers dragging through her cream. Indeed, no one else made her this wet. She spread her lips. "Here."

"Will it hurt?"

Abigail laughed at that. "Darling, it won't. And if it's not quite right, we'll try again, okay? There's more than one way to do this. Come." She lifted Minerva's hand back to her mouth again and licked the fingers, salty with her own cream. "I'll show you."

Together, they reached between Abigail's legs. Using Minerva's fingers, she tested her slit until she found the opening of her pussy. "Right there, darling," she whispered, leaning back on her elbows.

The woman had one hand on Abigail's thigh, the other at her opening. "You're so beautiful," she murmured and then her finger was sliding between the folds of Abigail's pussy and Abigail was gasping and Minerva was pulling out immediately. "Bad?"

"No, darling—so good. I want you inside of me." Right now, she was close to begging because Minerva, in her innocence and inexperience, was torturing her in an entirely different way. A good way, but it was driving Abigail absolutely insane.

"All right." Minerva gave her a crooked little smile, one stuck in the space between uncertainty and seduction, and then set her hands back. "Like this?"

Abigail's pussy gave willingly beneath Minerva's curious touches. "Yes," she murmured, biting her lip to keep from gasping at the sensations. She didn't want to scare Minerva off again. "That's it, Minerva. Oh, *yes*. Move in and...oh," she sighed as Minerva began to move her hand, stroking in and out of Abigail.

"Is this right?" she asked in an awestruck voice, her gaze fastened to where their bodies were joined.

"You feel good," Abigail assured her. "Does it feel right to you?"

"Yes," she whispered. "It's so…"

"*So*," Abigail agreed. "If you want to, you can add another finger."

"Can I?" But instead of waiting for the answer, Minerva did just that, filling Abigail even more.

"Yes," she hissed. This was something she didn't get with Opal. That was touching and mouths—but if anyone was going to put anything inside of anyone, it was going to be the paying customer and his rod.

Not Minerva's fingers, her other hand resting on Abigail's thigh. Not that look of lust—no, not even lust. The look in Minerva's eyes was something more than just the naked lust she saw at the Jeweled Ladies—it was deeper. There was more to the way Minerva stared down at her.

"Good?" Minerva asked. Abigail nodded, but that wasn't enough, apparently, because she asked, "Can it be better?"

"Touch me here," Abigail said, stroking her nub. Desire raced through her like a runaway coach, the horses threatening to break free. Her release was straining against her body and she was desperate. "Or kiss me. That's where I kissed you. But *something*, Minerva. I need something there."

"Oh, God." Minerva fell forward and kissed Abigail's mouth hard as she rubbed and thrust her fingers into Abigail's pussy and when Abigail's back arched off the bed, Minerva's mouth roughly came down on her breast and that was the final piece, the missing bit that sent Abigail over the edge and shattering into a million pieces.

"Ohh!" she groaned as the climax swept over her—stronger than any single joyful thing she'd ever felt in her life. She fell back onto the bed and immediately had to grab Minerva's hands away because the woman hadn't stopped her strokes and suddenly Abigail could feel too much. It was too intense and she was too wrung out with satisfaction.

"It's never been like that," she heard herself say, breathless and happy. She pulled Minerva down into her arms and kissed her long and hard.

"In a good way, I hope," the dear woman said with a smile.

"In the best way." They lay there for a long time, the air cooling around them as their breathing returned to normal.

So this was freedom. The emotions crashing through her were almost overwhelming. For all the men and women she'd lain with, she hadn't really known. It felt right that she should be discovering her true power with Minerva—because she did feel powerful. Not the kind of power that came from dominance, but from happiness. Because—for maybe the first time in her life—she was happy. Really, truly happy. She was lying in Minerva's arms, the smell of their sex perfuming the air. Minerva was teaching her to read. Abigail was sewing dresses for her. Soon...

Soon, she'd be able to leave Ebony White behind entirely. And when she did, she would be a new woman entirely.

"I wish..." She wished for all sorts of things she knew that she could never have.

This—Minerva—every night. A life that didn't involve men and money and sex with strangers, but dresses and beauty and quiet dinners and a bed big enough for two.

"So do I," Minerva whispered against her neck.

Her heart beating wildly all over again, she rolled and tucked Minerva against her before pulling the covers up over both of them. The smell of sex hung around the room, sweet and tart and completely unlike the way her room at the Jeweled Ladies smelled after a night of working.

Minerva pushed up onto her elbows and smiled down at Abigail. Oh, Abigail could still see the prickly schoolmarm in the corners of her eyes, the slant of her mouth—but this joyful woman was who she really was.

Then something shifted in Minerva's gaze, something Abigail could not ignore. Then she asked the question Abigail had been dreading. "Would you roll over for me?"

Chapter Fourteen

Abigail stiffened. She'd spend years positioning herself so that no one would get a good look at her back. "Why?"

"Please," Minerva said, sitting back on her heels. "I just...they're a part of you, you know? Those scars are part of your story. You may think them shameful, but to me..."

Abigail's cheeks burned. "They *are* shameful." The marks of her great mistake.

"But you survived," Minerva insisted. "They do not mark your weakness. They show your strength."

Her accent had changed as she spoke, the sounds of the North stronger. "I don't like people to look at them."

"Of course you don't," Minerva sniffed. "I don't like people to look at me at all. But I should hope..."

"Yes?" Even as she asked it, Abigail could feel the old fear churning in her stomach.

"I should hope I'm not like other people. Not to you."

That was a low blow—but Minerva was right. And really, wasn't that why they were here, lounging naked in bed?

"You survived," Minerva repeated softly.

"I know that," Abigail snapped. But she rolled over anyway. The sooner Minerva saw them, the sooner they could get this over with. "Just look, all right?"

"Oh," Minerva said, her voice even softer. Then she moved, a hand stroking over the scars. "I think not."

Before Abigail could process what she meant by that, something soft and sweet touched her back. The scars themselves—only a few of them were really awful, the ones that had gotten infected. Most of them were pale lines that were easy to ignore.

But the bad ones—those were the ones Minerva kissed. Abigail's body tensed at the touch but Minerva moved her lips over the knots of tissue and then began to smooth her hands over the rest of Abigail's back in soothing strokes and quite against her will, Abigail began to relax.

The few times either a gentleman caller or another Jewel—usually Opal—had gotten a good look at her back, they'd reacted with something that walked right between disgust and horror. And who could blame them? They were ugly to see, ugly to feel. They represented ugliness of spirit, too.

Minerva moved to straddle Abigail. Then she leaned down and continued to kiss the scars. Abigail could feel the weight of Minerva's breasts pressing against her back, warm and heavy.

And suddenly, Abigail was talking. The truth of the matter came pouring out of her like a jug that had been broken.

"None of them are from Mrs. Whithall except the one on my arm," she began. "She'd smack me when I did something she didn't like, but that was just an open

148

palm to the face or the ear. And never more than one at a time."

"How admirable of her," Minerva murmured, turning her attention to another scar. "An adult woman hitting a child? Even for a Catholic, that is a poor showing."

Abigail wouldn't have thought it possible, but she laughed at that. "She was a poor woman, in both her finances and her spirit. But it could have been worse."

"Do not say that as if that excuses her actions," Minerva said more sharply.

"No, I don't suppose it does." Although, in all honesty, she had always thought of it like that. She knew how much more awful her childhood could have been—oh, how she knew. But still…

Mrs. Whithall had hit her. Repeatedly. She had trained Abigail to accept that treatment of her person, which had made it harder for Abigail to see what a monster Mr. Dawson really had been because she had simply not known to expect anything else.

"Anyway, she died. A fever swept through Lexington and took her first. Then Miss Catherine took ill. She gave me my freedom, but I couldn't just leave her in her dying days. I stayed by her side until…" She swallowed and Minerva leaned her head against Abigail's shoulder. "That was early 1865."

"But…the Emancipation Proclamation?"

"Come now, Minerva." Abigail rested her head on her forearms. "Kentucky was a border state fighting on the Union's side. They got to keep their slaves. That Proclamation only freed slaves in Confederate states. Even an uneducated woman such as myself knew *that*."

The irony had been almost too much to bear. Miss Catherine had read Abigail from the newspaper about how the slaves were freed but not in Kentucky, because—as near as Abigail could figure—Kentucky supported the Union in the fight to free the slaves. What kind of sense did that make? It didn't.

"Go on," Minerva said, her hands stroking up and down Abigail's back.

She sighed, relaxing into Minerva's touch. The scars felt different from the rest of her skin but...

She could still feel Minerva's heat against her skin, smell Minerva's scent. And really, after she'd had Minerva splayed out before her, how was this different? "Mrs. Whithall's friends argued over who'd get to bring me into their household but Miss Catherine had signed the papers. I was free and I wasn't going to be anyone's servant ever again." That had been an intoxicating realization—Abigail had been able to say no. Those women had cajoled and demanded that she come with them, but none of them could make her do a single thing she didn't want to.

That feeling of power—it hadn't lasted. "I wanted my dress shop and I knew I'd never get it being someone else's ladies' maid. Then Mr. Dawson—we knew him from church. He had a tailor shop. He knew I'd done all the sewing for the Whithalls and he offered to set me up. He'd teach me the business and...and we'd be partners. After I earned back the cost of my education. I mean, it still would've been his name on the shop but he'd split the profits from my work with me and..."

God, it sounded so stupid now. She'd agreed to his terms for the apprenticeship. She'd work for him without pay and in exchange, he'd teach her to read and to keep the books.

Seven years. She'd signed her life away for seven years because she'd dared to hope that this was the way to get her shop. Dawson had used her innocence and her hope against her.

But she hadn't known who he really was, not back then. He was a gentleman who'd called upon Mrs. Whithall from time to time, who'd always brought a special treat for Miss Catherine and had said kind things about the dresses Abigail had sewn. Mrs. Whithall had spoken warmly of him.

"He didn't keep his word," Minerva guessed. Her fingers worked at Abigail's shoulders and only then did Abigail realize how tense she'd gotten.

"No. The changes were so small at first that I didn't even realize what was happening." She took a deep breath, her eyes stinging. She didn't want to cry. This was exactly why she tried not to think of that time. It left her with such a sense of hopelessness. How dare she think she could ever get her shop? How dare she think she could amount to anything?

"You know what they say," Abigail went on, swallowing around the lump in her throat. "You put a frog in boiling water, it'll just jump out. But you put it in cold water and slowly heat it up and you've got frog soup. And I was the frog. By the time I realized what happening, it was too late. I was trapped, completely at his mercy. And that's when he showed me who he *really* was." She began to cry in earnest.

"Oh, my dear girl," Minerva whispered. She covered Abigail's back with her body, her weight warm and comforting. Minerva moved Abigail's hair aside and pressed a kiss to the side of her neck. "It wasn't your fault."

"It was," she insisted. "I was such a fool, Minerva. God, such a fool. Mrs. Whithall was no saint but she'd never let anyone use me like he did. And I let him. *I let him*," she wept.

That was the thing that had always hurt the worst—if only she'd tried harder, she could have kept Dawson from crossing that line from demanding supervisor to abusive demon. She should have tried harder to escape. She should have done anything but lie there and take it.

But she hadn't. Why hadn't she?

"*No*, Abigail. That's a lie. You were not a fool," she insisted when Abigail shook her head in disagreement. "You merely trusted the wrong person. The crime—and all responsibility for it—is his. It was not your fault. You were innocent."

"I should have tried harder to get free," she whispered. "But I was so scared of him and I didn't know where I could go. He promised he'd find me and I'd messed up so bad..."

"That doesn't make his actions your fault." She slid off to the side and made Abigail look at her. "My family—we were a waystation on the Underground Railroad. My father had a cart with a false bottom and we'd get all manner of people trying to escape the bonds of enslavement and it was never their fault. But almost to a person, they had a measure of guilt to their stories. They should have run sooner. They shouldn't have left a loved one behind. They should have fought harder for their families. Those people—they were risking everything on the hope that there was a better life out there, just like you did. They sat at our table and ate our meals with us and poured out their hearts and it was never, ever their fault. It was always those poor excuses for humanity who thought it their divine right to own and subjugate a race of people and I sincerely hope those people burn in Hell."

It was the most fervent thing she'd ever heard Minerva say. "I know that, but—"

But she'd signed the papers with Dawson. She'd moved into the small room—the closet, really—in the shop, the one with no windows and a lock on the outside of the door. She'd put herself into his hands and then been unable to get away.

Minerva cut off her protestations. "It wasn't your fault, dearest Abigail. Do not feel guilty for things done to you against your will because that was never your responsibility to bear. It wasn't."

For some reason, that made Abigail cry all the harder. "I'm sorry," she blubbered. "I've never told anyone about this."

"Don't apologize either, dear girl," Minerva said, her voice surprisingly gentle as she pulled Abigail into her arms. "Your pain is real. You did what you thought was best and then you survived the worst of it. That's what counts. You survived, my dear girl. You're here and you're whole and that's all behind you now. I only hope that I can take some of the burden from you."

Oh. She'd no idea that was something she needed—to let someone else carry the weight on her shoulders right until Minerva had said it. She'd thought she needed her shop, security. She'd dared to dream of one day finding someone who she could willingly share her bed with.

But someone who could look at the marks Dawson left her with and not recoil in disgust? Someone who could hear her story and not think her the greatest fool who ever lived?

She curled into Minerva's arms and sobbed. She lost all track of time as Minerva stroked her hair and held her close and whispered soft words of love.

She didn't cry. She didn't beg. Both were emotions that signified weakness and that weakness had always been used against her.

But here? As her tears dried, she felt lighter than she had in…well, since Miss Catherine had signed the papers giving Abigail her freedom.

Eventually, Abigail was able to look up. She'd cried a small puddle into Minerva's shoulders and Abigail was certain her eyes and nose were beyond all hope. "Thank you," she said, trying to smile. She didn't make it, but she felt better anyway. "I didn't expect you to understand."

Minerva snorted as she cupped Abigail's cheek and wiped away an errant tear. It was not a ladylike sound. "I am difficult. Not heartless."

A tremulous smile took hold of Abigail's mouth. "You're not really difficult. Just…prickly. When you're nervous, mostly. Which," she added, drawing her arms back around Minerva's waist, their skin warm against each other, "you're not right now."

"No, I suppose I am not." They lay there for a while, enjoying the intimacy of silence. "May I ask how you escaped that horrible man?"

"Oh, that. From what I understand, one of the ladies I sewed a gown for—she recognized what was happening. I believe Mistress said she had escaped a violent husband? In any case, she contacted the Jeweled Ladies."

"She wanted you to become a Jewel? I fail to see how that wasn't just trading one form of servitude for another."

"No, no. You don't understand. Mistress—she rescues people. Like Nonoci?" At Minerva's blank stare, she said, "Turquoise Sky? You saw her in the dry-goods store, didn't you?"

"Wait—she said she'd rescued that Native girl from...well, from a church."

"She did. She does that sort of thing all the time." Minerva gaped at her as if she'd suddenly sprouted wings. "She keeps it quiet, so you mustn't tell anyone. And very few of us wind up as Jewels."

"I am...well. I am stunned. I always thought..."

Abigail grinned. "Everyone does. But deep down, Mistress is one of the kindest, most fair people I've ever known." Except for the part where she hadn't taught Abigail to read.

She'd been with Mistress for almost two years. Why had it taken so long for her to engage the services of Minerva?

"Anyway," Abigail went on, feeling much better now. She had to wonder why she'd kept this story bottled up inside of her. "Mistress swept into that shop, demanding the finest of dresses—money was no object. Mr. Dawson bent over backward to give her what she wanted."

It wasn't as if Abigail had never seen fancy ladies before. Her time in the shop had shown her that the Whithall women had been at the edge of genteel poverty. But Mistress had waltzed into Dawson's shop like—well, like Mistress. Satins and silks and gems hanging from her neck and ears, huge feathers in her hat. Everything about her had screamed money and Dawson had been only too happy to listen.

"She came for you?"

"She did. Over three separate fittings, she bossed him around and then, when his back was turned, she'd do these little things—touch my cheek, pull the back of my dress down. She was looking for the signs of abuse, but I just thought..."

Abigail had thought there was a sexual interest there and Mistress had been very beautiful.

Then, on her third visit, Mistress had winked at Abigail and smiled that beautiful smile and Abigail had been filled with the feeling that things were going to be all right. It had been impossible to explain then and was no less impossible now.

Abigail sat up, her legs crossed. "It was glorious. On her third visit, Mr. Dawson had his back turned to her to get at a bolt of fabric and she pulled out a gun. She pointed it right at his stones and informed him that I was coming with her and if word of his actions ever again reached her ears, next time he wouldn't keep all his body parts."

"Good heavens," Minerva murmured in shock.

Dawson had wet his pants. Even now—and although it probably made her a bad person—she found an intense amount of satisfaction in that. It was her favorite memory of Dawson. "While she had the gun on him, she told me to take whatever I wanted and that we were leaving and do you know what? That man had the nerve to tell me I didn't have to go with her."

Minerva laughed, although it was not a sound filled with joy. "Did he really think he was doing you a favor?"

"I suppose. As I was gathering up my things—I only had enough for a small bundle—two men came into the store. Mistress had hired them to make sure Dawson didn't follow us, I believe. We left, so I never did know what happened to him afterwards."

"If he did not suffer on this earth, at least he will suffer mightily in the hereafter for his sins," Minerva asked.

"Oh, knowing Mistress as I do, I would wager that he suffered." In all honesty, she wouldn't be surprised if the two men had burned the shop to the ground. "She brought me back here and told me she'd be happy to get me a place as a maid or even as a seamstress's apprentice. But I couldn't risk that again and she made it clear—whoring paid well. I could have everything I'd ever wanted for just a few years of my time, plus plenty of practice sewing for the Jewels. And since I was already ruined, I thought why not?"

Minerva looked like she wanted to argue with this sentiment—but then thought better of it. "So learning to read—was that the final thing you needed?"

"Indeed. You could come with me, when I go."

"With you? You mean…" she swallowed. "Leave Brimstone?"

Abigail groaned inwardly. They'd agreed that this was a little bit of loving for just a little while. What existed between them didn't come with any guarantees. As eager a student as Minerva was, she was committed to her position as schoolteacher here. "Never mind. I wasn't thinking." She pulled Minerva in closer. She would have kept her mouth shut—if it hadn't been for that soft "So do I" Minerva had whispered earlier.

There had been something in those three little words—words Abigail could read and write now. Something that had sparked hope in her chest.

But hope was dangerous because it meant you wanted something and that something could be taken away from you.

She'd spent her whole childhood hoping to learn to read, only to have that denied her. She'd spent her adolescence hoping to be freed. She'd spent every single moment in Mr. Dawson's dress shop hoping that it was all just a nightmare and that she'd wake up. She'd spent the last two years once again hoping to read and once again having it denied to her.

Hoping was nothing but a heartbreak waiting to happen.

But despite all of that, Abigail couldn't help but hope that maybe Minerva would want to be with her. No, not even that—that Minerva would take a risk to be with her. Because it would be a risk, going off into the west and starting over again—for both of them.

The silence stretched.

She shouldn't have said anything. She squeezed her eyes shut just in case she did anything stupid, like cry over something she knew damned well she could never have. Hope was bad enough when she kept it to herself. But sharing it gave the other person power over her dreams.

But even with her eyes closed, she could see a neat little bedroom with papered walls and a small fireplace for cold nights. She could see a looking glass and a wardrobe bursting with pretty dresses and a hand-stitched quilt over a wide bed.

It would be perfect.

She shouldn't dream of such things.

Then Minerva moved, her hand stroking over Abigail's hair. "When are you thinking of going?"

And that traitorous hope flared bright in her soul because if she could just help Minerva see that future...

"As soon as I have enough money saved up. Maybe even this spring, when travelling is easier. I hear Virginia City's got a lot of money, but it doesn't matter as long as there are ladies who can afford nice dresses." She swallowed again. "And if there are ladies who need dresses, I'm sure there'd be children who need to learn to read and count and such."

Minerva was quiet again and Abigail kept talking. "Starting over—it's a big thing and if I have references from proper ladies...I mean, I'll always sew for the brothels. That's where the good money is. But," she said, pushing up onto her side and staring down at Minerva, "I want to have a respectable business. You'll help me, won't you?"

A look of pain flittered across Minerva's face. "How? I want to, Abigail. You know I do. That's the reason I agreed to tutor you in the first place. But..."

Her voice trailed off and she shuddered—and not in a good way.

"All you'd have to do is wear the dresses I make you and—"

Minerva made a face. "You're making me *another* dress? I can't just wear the skirt and shirt?"

Abigail smiled patiently. "That's a fine everyday

159

outfit. I'm actually making you another set. No, I *am*," she said firmly as Minerva started to protest. "Because I want to, darling. But I'm working on a proper dress for you. You're going to look amazing in it."

Oddly, these words didn't seem to reassure Minerva. "And then what?" she said, looking panicked.

Abigail did the only thing she could think of to calm the woman down—she kissed her. When she pulled back, she stared down at this beautiful woman, her face knit with worry. "All you'd have to do is tell people I made the dress. That's it." Emmy was organizing everything else.

For a moment, she thought Minerva would balk, she really did. But then Minerva's hands cupped her face and she kissed Abigail back and said, "For you. Only for you, my dear girl."

And that was all it took. A wild kind of hope took hold of Abigail. Maybe this would work out. She could get her shop and keep Minerva and together, they'd make a life.

A real life, one she wanted. One she fought for. One she didn't wait for anyone to give her because she knew the world would never give her anything.

"Don't worry," she told Minerva as the kisses grew longer and deeper. "It'll be fine. You'll see."

She hoped she was right.

Chapter Fifteen

The next night, it was harder than ever for Abigail to dress in Ebony White's black dresses and clasp Ebony White's jet jewels around her neck and pile Ebony White's hair high on her head and plaster Ebony White's smile on her face and go to the parlor of the Jeweled Ladies and sit in Ebony White's chair and wait for the men.

She never had to wait long.

There had been a time when she...well, she'd never liked this. But it had been easier to do this because no matter how much she did or did not enjoy her customers, it was always better than it had been before. If she gave herself away, then the fact that Mr. Dawson had taken her against her will didn't...

It didn't matter as much. Sex wasn't special, just something to get through—and all the better if she could get paid for it. Her virtue wasn't a treasure stolen, but an inconvenience she was well rid of.

Here, she was treated with respect and dignity.

At least that's what she'd convinced herself of. And then, when she went upstairs, she thought of her dress shop. That had been the most important thing. The shop. It was the key to her happiness.

Once, it had been all she wanted. But now?

"Miss White," Roy Griffith said, bowing before her. "You are radiant this evening, as usual."

She smiled up at Roy and batted her eyelashes. Roy was one of her regulars and perhaps the customer she liked best. He was young and good-looking and he owned the Golden Star hotel, which made him quite well off. Plus, he was unmarried. Too many of her customers were married to white women and got a perverse pleasure out of fucking a black whore on the side.

Maybe her father had been like that? She didn't know. She had no memory of either of her parents. Just Mrs. Whithall. Just Miss Catherine.

Too much of her life and her history was a blank.

"Mr. Griffith," she cooed, just like she'd been taught, batting her lashes at him.

"May I have the pleasure of your company this evening?" He asked the same thing twice a week.

He wasn't so generous that he paid for the whole evening—but he was still a comfort. He was kind to her. He kissed her on the mouth and took the time to ready her body for his, instead of just shoving and pounding. He was affectionate, even. And he never made her feel less of a woman because she was Ebony White. Why, when they met on the street, he greeted her by name and often stopped long enough to compliment her on her dress or tell her how much he was looking forward to their next meeting.

In other words, he'd always been the best of all possible outcomes.

And despite all that, she didn't love him. She never had. Maybe she couldn't.

Because he wasn't Minerva.

He held out his hand. She looked honored by his request—as usual—and took his hand. "I'm always glad to see you, sir," she said and, until the time she'd started loving on Minerva, that had been true.

How was she supposed to do this now? Because, as she led Roy upstairs to her room, she wasn't able to conjure up her shop or the fabrics or the happy customers twirling in her gowns.

All she could see was Minerva, her fingers sliding into Abigail's body, her cream flooding Abigail's mouth, her cries of pleasure filling Abigail's ears.

She knew—*knew*—after months and months of Roy's attentions, that she wouldn't find that pleasure here.

He undressed her, kissing along her shoulders and tits as she undid his buttons and shoved his trousers down. She made sure to keep her back pointed away from him as she fell onto the bed, trying to find the smiles and sighs she used to make a man feel like he was doing a good job.

But as Roy's hands stroked her pussy and spread her wide, she just wanted to cry. He fit his sheathed rod to her and began to thrust and it just wasn't the same. She couldn't think of her dress shop. She couldn't think of anything but Minerva and how this wasn't what she wanted. Not anymore.

It took everything she had not to cry.

After Roy was finished, they lay together, his head buried against her bosom as he panted.

And suddenly she needed to say something. She didn't love this man, but she did like and respect him. She needed to say something out loud and make it real.

"I'm learning to read."

He looked up at her, surprised. "You don't know how?"

She shook her head as he slipped free of her body. She sighed with relief.

"I would have taught you."

"You would've?" She wasn't sure she believed that. It was the sort of thing that was easy to say, harder to do.

Still, though, he might mean it. He rolled to his side and wrapped his arms around her. "Have you ever thought about leaving the Jeweled Ladies behind?"

Constantly. "I don't plan on living the rest of my life here," she replied truthfully enough.

He traced a finger over her nipple and she knew he'd have her again before he tugged his pants back on and paid her for her time. She wondered what had happened to inspire this performance tonight—usually he was one and done.

"I can't marry you, you know. It's not legal."

Whites and coloreds couldn't marry anywhere that she knew of. "I know. And I would never ask that of you."

He propped himself up on his elbow and looked down at her, a surprising tenderness in his eyes. "I could still take you away from all this."

Something dropped in her stomach and belatedly, she realized it might be fear. "How?"

"I own the Golden Star. I could set you up—you could live there. We could see each other whenever we wanted. You wouldn't have to do *this* with anyone else."

She closed her eyes, trying to picture the life he was offering her. She would be his mistress, exclusive.

She could live in a nice hotel. It wouldn't be bad. She knew that.

But...she'd be completely dependent on him. People would talk about the black woman he kept. Would she even be able to eat in the dining room, or would she have to take her meals in the kitchen or her room? And when he grew tired of her or he decided to marry a suitable woman—what would happen to her?

No. She would not be at any man's mercy ever again. Not even a man as nice as Roy.

"That'd be a no, then," he said, a note of sadness in his voice before his head came to rest on her shoulder. She lifted her hand and stroked his head to comfort him. That, at least, wasn't an act.

"I can't."

"I don't care what they'd say," he defended.

"But your future wife might and I can't do that to you, Roy."

He was silent, his finger still tracing a path around her nipple. "It's not someone else, is it? I can take better care of you than any of your other customers can. You must know that."

"I do. And it means so much to me that you'd offer. But I can't." Because saying *yes* to Roy would mean more than giving up her shop. It'd mean giving up Minerva. "I wouldn't even consider an offer from anyone else," she assured him. It was the least she could do. "You mean more to me than that."

She moved her hands over his body, doing her best to make him happy. It was sweet of him to offer but...

No man would control her fate. Not ever again.

So she let him mount her again and this time, instead of thinking of her shop and fabrics and fashion plates, she thought of Minerva, her innocence and lust and curiosity all rolled together.

The sooner she could get away from Ebony White…

If only she could get Minerva to come with her.

Her new dream carried her through the rest of her night.

*

Minerva was beyond nervous. *Nervous* was too small a word for the stark terror she felt coursing through her body, knotting her stomach and making this corset—the corset Abigail had made for her—far too restrictive. How was she supposed to breathe in this thing?

This entire dress—and this was the dress, not the skirt and shirtwaist and jacket—was ridiculous. Tight and…and fashionable. The wool was not a dark navy, but a vibrant royal blue, so blue it was almost purple. It was a color that was designed to catch the eye.

Abigail knew her well enough not to have added a bustle under the dress, but she had layered this sumptuous fabric so that it was almost a mock bustle in the back, draped over Minerva's bottom in a way that was guaranteed to draw the eye. And in the front? Above a few flounces at the hem, Abigail had a row of tiny bows in a soft cream color.

Bows. On the schoolteacher's dress.

The collar came up high on the back of her neck and that was a relief. Even though the collar was lower in front, it still came up a respectable way. But the buttons up the front of the dress were tiny pearls.

Pearls. On the schoolteacher's dress.

Minerva stood behind the door of the schoolhouse, willing herself to do...something. To turn around and put on her regular Saturday dress. Or even the more respectable skirt and jacket outfit.

Or she could open the door and walk outside in this finery. Because it was Saturday. The day she did what little shopping she could afford to do in Brimstone.

At their lesson on Thursday, Abigail had given her a new bonnet, a simple straw one with a lovely blue ribbon to match the dress perfectly. There was a bow on the side of the bonnet. There was no overlooking that bow.

She could do this. She could open this door and walk down the hill to Main Street and she could go into the dry-goods store and play her part.

The door didn't open.

No, that was untrue. She, Miss Minerva Krenshaw, didn't open the door.

She tried to convince her feet to move. In all honesty, compared to what Abigail wore, the whole outfit wasn't even that special. Her arms were covered. She had a pair of gloves on—new ones of soft kid leather. The dress was buttoned up to her neck.

But it was the first new bonnet she had had in over ten years and her head felt heavy under the weight of it. The straw stood stiff, instead of flopping down into her face and bouncing off the rim of her spectacles. The corset made breathing difficult. And the color...

People would notice. If she had learned anything wearing the skirt and jacket over the last few weeks, people would compliment her on the new dress and bonnet. They would look at her and, in all honesty, Minerva was terrified of what they might see. Absolutely *terrified.*

Because what if they could see the truth? Oh, Abigail had promised that no one could see what was in her heart. *Promised* that no one would know that she lusted after one of Mistress's Jewels.

But Minerva knew the truth. She was a terrible actress, a terrible liar. She always had been.

People would look at her for the clothing. They would keep looking at her for the guilt on her face. She might as well walk around with a giant red *A* pinned to her chest.

But she had promised Abigail. The dear girl had gone to so much trouble to make her new things. And she had been right. Now that Minerva was getting used to the way the new corset fit, it was more comfortable than the old one. Being able to take the jacket off when she got warm instead of miserably sweating in a most unladylike fashion was also a relief. She was able to move and teach fully without pulling in the shoulders of the shirt.

But it wasn't just the fit. The clothes made her feel different in other ways. It was ridiculous, but she felt like… Like when she was wearing these things, that she stood a little taller. Which was a problem, because being even taller than she already was would mean that more people would be looking at her.

God, she didn't know if she could do this.

She was under no illusions. She was the bait in a trap waiting to be sprung at the dry-goods store and the townsfolk were the prey.

She wouldn't do it.

But she'd promised Abigail...

So she amended her earlier thought. She wouldn't do it for anyone but Abigail.

She opened the door, stepped outside, and began to walk.

It began almost immediately. "I adore that color," Miss Cynthia Hobbs, the banker's daughter, said as Minerva passed. Which was good because Miss Hobbs was exactly the kind of lady Abigail wanted to sew dresses for. She bought new dresses every season and followed all the latest fashions, in addition to having a lovely figure that made all those dresses look beautiful.

But Minerva couldn't stand here in the middle of the street and have that conversation. And thankfully, she didn't have to. Instead of asking Minerva about the dress, Miss Hobbs turned to her father and said, "I want a dress that color, Daddy."

Minerva hurried away before anyone could ask a question. Which, unfortunately, brought her closer to the dry-goods store much faster than she wanted.

The moment she crossed the threshold, she wished she'd stayed in the schoolhouse because the store was overflowing with people—dozens of people, all doing their shopping for the week. Ranch hands and mothers with children, cooks and wives—it seemed like the whole town was crammed into this store. There was barely room to move and for a second, Minerva considered just...slipping off the way she'd come.

She didn't get the chance. "Miss Krenshaw!" crowed Mrs. Snyder from behind the counter. "Is that really *you*?"

A hush fell over the crowd. All eyes turned to her. It was oppressive.

Minerva tried to smile but her mouth wasn't working. It didn't feel like *anything* was working. "Good day to you, Mrs. Snyder."

The wide woman gave her a wide smile. "Well, aren't you just the prettiest thing, all made up? If you don't mind me asking, where did you get that lovely dress?" She drew out the syllable on lovely. *Love-lee.*

Minerva's throat closed around the words—the words she had promised she would say. The words that would publicly identify Miss Ebony White of the Jeweled Ladies as a seamstress, skilled not only in risqué evening gowns and daring corsetry, but a woman capable of sewing a dress for even the most strict, proper woman in town. A woman capable of sewing dresses for the banker's daughter, even.

Everyone was looking at her. The edges of her vision began to go blurry and dark.

"I agree," came another voice, soft and seductive. Mistress's voice. Minerva wheeled around on legs that didn't feel like they could hold up her weight anymore and found herself staring at the decadent bosom and glimmering jewels of the finest whore in town. "Miss Krenshaw, that is quite a proper ensemble. So demure! Why, I could see any woman in town walking around in such a respectable outfit. Wherever did you get it?"

And there—in the middle of a narrow tunnel vision, just behind Mistress's shoulder, Minerva saw Abigail, standing with Mrs. Raymond Dupree and another Jewel, all wearing the finest of finery. Abigail had sewed all those dresses, no doubt.

Abigail was dressed in her finest gown—the

black velvet, sumptuous and infinitely touchable, clinging to every curve. Curves Minerva had touched. Her lips were painted today and jet beads decorated her neck and her bosom. A bosom that Minerva had kissed. Everything was designed to catch the eye and make people look at her. Minerva had never been able to look away.

Why were they all staring at Minerva instead?

"Get out of my way," came yet another voice—harsh, male. Judgmental. Oh, *God.*

But her prayers were not going to be answered, not today. Not when Judge Gerard Hobson pushed his way through the ring of onlookers. "I might've known," he sneered at Mistress, "that *you* would be in the middle of this mess." He looked around. "Why are all you idiots just standing around here? Don't you have something to be doing?"

The words felt like a cannonball blowing a hole in Minerva's mind. She was completely paralyzed now. She couldn't move. She couldn't *breathe.*

Perhaps it wasn't a surprise when Mistress came to her rescue. "Your Honor," she all but purred. "We were just noticing that Miss Krenshaw has a new dress and we were eagerly awaiting her to tell us where she had it made. It's women's fashion," she went on in a dismissive tone, slanting a hard look at the judge. "I doubt *you* would care for it one way or the other."

And just when Minerva thought she couldn't take another moment, it got worse because then Judge Hobson turned his icy gray eyes to her as if he had just noticed her for the first time in all of her eight years in the town of Brimstone. "Who?" he said, as if he had just stepped in something foul.

She couldn't look away. Her vision narrowed again until she all could see was the disdain on his face. She had worked with this man, supported him in elections. He had wanted to get rid of the brothels and the saloons. He had wanted to make Brimstone a God-fearing town and she had done everything to advance that cause.

She had tried to get rid of Abigail.

But the way he was looking at her right now? There was no hiding. He could *tell*. He could probably smell Abigail on her, the way his nostrils flared like that.

"Really, Judge Hobson," Mistress said in a stronger tone now. "There is no need to terrify the schoolteacher."

And then Mistress moved into her pinpoint of vision, a comforting look on her face. She reached out an arm to draw Minerva to her side. "Pay no mind to the judge, dear. Tell us where you got that lovely dress?" It was more of an order that time.

Minerva's gaze swung wildly round the room. The judge's lip curled in disgust. Other people were watching Mistress be nice to her—*associate* with her. Everyone was staring at her like she was being led to the gallows and would soon dance on the end of a rope for their entertainment.

Somehow, through it all, her gaze found Abigail's. Well. At least there was someone else in this room who looked as Minerva felt. Terrified. *Horrified.*

Abigail…

She was supposed to tell this group of people that the woman they only thought of as a whore was more than that. She was a woman with a plan. One with talent and determination. Minerva was supposed to tell everyone that Abigail Whithall was a dressmaker of the first order.

"Dear?" Mistress prodded, her smile tightening. "Who made the dress?"

But if Minerva did that, everyone would *know*. At the very least, they would know that she had spent time in the company of prostitutes. Mistress being nice to her? In public?

Then, in an alarming moment of realization, she hit upon a fact that she hadn't seen before. Abigail herself had said that Mistress paid for all the fabrics she could want so that every dollar Abigail earned went toward her shop.

Minerva was wearing clothes Abigail had made.

Minerva was wearing fabric Mistress had paid for.

Her position rested entirely on her reputation.

She was stunned to hear the words come out of her own mouth, equally stunned that she was unable to stop them. "I made it myself."

Abigail gasped, a hand coming to her perfect chest as the lie rippled out through the crowd. Her friends closed ranks around her, a wall of temptation. God, why had Minerva been so tempted?

"I'm sorry?" Mistress said, her gaze turning hard in a heartbeat.

Dear God, what had she done? What was she *still doing*? Minerva opened her mouth to take back the lie—lying was surely a sin that could not be excused with flowery talk of love and hope and happiness.

But just then, a whisper reached her ears.

173

Somewhere in this store, overflowing with townspeople buying flour and nails and peppermint sticks and needles, someone whispered, "Why is the schoolteacher talking to *that* woman?"

This was all it would take to destroy her reputation. No more than a whisper would have her relieved of her position as the schoolteacher in this town. She would be without a job, without a place to live. She didn't have much but she had her reputation.

She was about to lose it. She was about to lose everything.

She had no choice. "Madam, unhand me, if you please. I assure you that wherever I get my clothes, it is of no concern to you."

Mistress narrowed her eyes. Minerva could almost hear her say, *we had a deal.*

Minerva had just broken the deal. Everything that Abigail wanted had hinged on being respectable enough to open up a dress shop and sew for proper ladies, not just soiled doves.

Her mouth opened again as she struggled for some way to right the wrong she was actively doing. But again came that whisper, although it was a different speaker. "Those women shouldn't be bothering her. It's not right."

No, nothing about this was right. There was really only one thing to do.

Minerva turned on her heel and walked out of the store.

Chapter Sixteen

D ear?"
Abigail started at the voice. She was surprised to see Mistress standing next to her. She was equally surprised to see that she was standing in her room at the Jeweled Ladies. She didn't remember coming back here from the dry-goods store.

But she must have because there she was, Mistress in front of her, her brow etched with concern. "I haven't seen that look on your face since… Well, since I found you." Moving slowly, Mistress reached up and unpinned the hat from Abigail's head. "Come to the office, dear."

Abigail managed to shake her head. "I don't think…"

"Come to the office," Mistress repeated, more firmly this time. She looped her arm around Abigail's shoulder and guided her out of the room and down the stairs to the small office at the end of the hallway that looked out onto Main Street.

Most of the Jeweled Ladies was done in elaborate papers and gilded mirrors and all sorts of finery. But Mistress's office was spare. There was a row of cabinets that lined one wall and a massive desk angled so that Mistress could both keep an eye on the street and the door. Before that were two worn leather chairs. It was into one of these that Mistress settled Abigail. Instead of moving to the other side of the desk as she had every other time Abigail had been in this room, Mistress sat next to Abigail and took one of her hands. "You are upset," she began.

"It's fine," Abigail lied. "I'm not surprised."

Mistress gave her quite a look. "You are? I only ask because you seem a *little* surprised."

Abigail would've laughed if she could've. But the laugh would mean that she could feel and feeling would mean that she could hurt. "She's terrified of crowds. She doesn't like people looking at her. It was too much for her."

Maybe deep down, she had known. Miss Minerva Krenshaw had existed outside of the public's awareness for so long that to be suddenly thrust into the middle of a scene like that—no, Abigail wasn't surprised that she had turned and ran. In fact, she was having trouble even being upset with Minerva. Abigail understood why she had done that. She did, really.

No, the person whom Abigail was most upset with was herself. She had known this would happen. Oh, maybe not this exact turn of events. But she had allowed herself to be swept up in Emmy's grand plans to build Abigail's reputation. She had allowed herself to hope that she was worth something more to Minerva, more than clandestine meetings and whispered affections.

Abigail had allowed herself to hope that she was worth something at all.

"You defend her," Mistress said, her voice containing a note of surprise. "You really do love her, don't you?"

176

That was too much. Abigail dropped her gaze into her lap, where she was surprised to see that her fingers were making a proper mess of the neat folds of her skirt.

"I can go talk to her. I'm sure she does feel terrible, but we had a deal and she did not honor it."

"No," Abigail said softly. Because she couldn't see how that would make anything better, Mistress walking up to the schoolhouse in broad daylight banging on the door, demanding entry so that she could harangue Minerva.

Minerva, who had always been perfectly clear that she valued her reputation and her position above all else.

Minerva, who had spent ten years hiding from the simple truth that she loved women instead of men. No, not even women. She had been sweet on one girl a long time ago.

Abigail's mistake was in hoping that Minerva could love anyone at all. Even her.

All of Abigail's life, she had been at the mercy of other people. She'd never had a choice in the matter, until Minerva. Minerva had not taken Abigail's power from her—Abigail had given it freely. She'd given her heart to the woman.

Hope was nothing but a heartache waiting to happen and Abigail didn't have any more to wait.

"We should have arranged it differently," Mistress was saying. "Perhaps Cynthia Hobbs…"

"No," Abigail repeated more insistently. Because now that the shock of Minerva's betrayal was wearing off, she was able to see more clearly.

There was no place for her in Brimstone. Not anymore. Maybe there never had been.

It was time to go.

She looked at Mistress. Worry was not attractive on her. There was something almost maternal about her in this moment that skirted Abigail's awareness.

Mistress always called the Jeweled Ladies her *girls*. She gave them new names and new clothes and trained them in the arts of seduction and negotiation. She enforced rules. She spoke of the power that went with having control of your own life. And Abigail had believed her. Like a fool, she had followed Mistress into this life with little more than hope to light her way.

"Why didn't you teach me to read?"

Mistress reacted as if Abigail had slapped her. She sucked in a gasp of air through her teeth and went pale. "What?"

Because once, Abigail had had a kindly white woman who was almost a mother to her. And the woman had *owned* her. That woman had refused to teach her to read, refused to free her even on her deathbed.

Mrs. Whithall had kept Abigail a slave because she could. Because she could hide her hideousness behind the veneer of polite and kind.

"Why didn't you teach me to read?" Abigail said again, more slowly this time. "I've been here for two years. Minerva taught me to read in a few months, a few hours a week. It wouldn't have cost you a thing to teach me to read. So why didn't you?"

Part of her mind screamed that Mistress was not the same as Mrs. Whithall. But underneath that mask of caring, was Mistress really that different at all?

The older woman stood, putting space between

178

them. "When I found you, I could see that you were strong. Strong enough to hold onto yourself in the face of servitude. That's a special gift, you know. Not everyone could keep their hearts whole in the face of what you suffered. So I brought you here."

"So you could keep me? How is this any different from how *he* kept me? How is this any different from how Mrs. Whithall kept me? You didn't teach me to read because you knew that I couldn't leave!"

Mistress looked down at her for a long moment and an old part of Abigail wanted to cringe and brace for the slap across the face. But it didn't come. Instead, Mistress came around and sat next to Abigail again. "I didn't teach you," she said slowly, "because I didn't want you to stay forever. I thought that, perhaps if I taught you how to read, you might feel indebted to me. You might feel obliged to stay. And you are not. I would rather have you hate me and leave of your own free will than have you stay because you owed me."

Abigail stared at her, her mouth open to her chest. "*What?*"

"You have come so far, Abigail. You have become a lady who knows her worth and knows how to get what she wants." Mistress looked almost tender. "You have enough money saved up for your shop now. You've put the past behind you as best you can. I think it's time that you move on and because I think that, I engaged the schoolteacher to teach you to read."

Abigail understood the words. She could probably even spell most of them correctly on the first try. But she couldn't make any sense out of what Mistress was saying. "You want me to *hate* you?"

"Of course not," Mistress answered quickly. "I care

179

for you deeply. I don't want you to be Ebony White forever. There's more to your life. I know it and you know it. I didn't want you to settle for this life like I did."

And that didn't make any sense, either. Mistress was one of the richest, most powerful women in town—possibly in the state of Texas. She had enough reach to go all the way to Lexington and rescue a poor girl.

She had purposely not taught Abigail how to read so that one day, Abigail would push her away.

Well, it worked. "You want me to go."

Mistress notched an eyebrow at her. "Actually, I don't. But I think you should, anyway." She leaned over and extracted of slip of paper from the desk. As Abigail watched, Mistress wrote on it. When she was done, she waved it in the air so that the ink dried and then handed it over to Abigail. "I know you thought about San Francisco, but I think you should start in Virginia City. I know a madam there who could use a good seamstress. She says there's quite a demand from ladies of all kinds for suitable dresses."

Abigail eyed the paper nervously. "What is it?"

For the first time in a very long time, Mistress smiled. A wide, friendly smile, the kind that would leave wrinkles and therefore, the kind that Abigail did not see very often. "Why don't you read it and tell me?"

Abigail snatched the paper away, her cheeks burning at that thinly veiled taunt. She stared down at the rectangle of paper and saw that it was a bank draft. From the First Macon County Bank. Made out for... "This is a thousand dollars."

"It is payment for services rendered as a dressmaker. You have done fine work and I'm only sorry that other people's prejudices have kept you limited."

Pain flared at the reference to Minerva but she pushed it away and stared down at the bank draft. Mistress had never said anything about paying her for the dresses. Mistress had not taught her to read.

Mistress was giving her a huge sum of money in addition to the savings Abigail had in the bank. Mistress was giving her a letter of reference and guaranteeing her clients in Virginia City.

Mistress had saved her from Mr. Dawson.

"What happened to Dawson?"

She lifted a shoulder but didn't meet Abigail's gaze. "I'm sure he got what he deserved."

She wasn't going to tell. But maybe Abigail didn't *want* to know. "So that's it?"

Mistress nodded. "I'll hire a coach and a guide for you. There's some wild territory between here and Virginia City," she explained. "You can be gone within a week. Unless you'd prefer to stay. Roy Griffith…"

Abigail shook her head. "He's not for me."

Mistress gave her a measured look. "No man will ever be good enough for you, will they?" Abigail's cheeks heated as Mistress went on, "All I ask is that you write me from time to time." She looked at Abigail, a small smile tucked away in the corner of her mouth. "I'd like to see a letter from you, letting me know how you are."

Abigail's eyes stung unexpectedly. She stood, trying to get control over her emotions. "And what of Minerva?"

Mistress leaned back in her chair, looking thoughtful. "What of her?"

Abigail truly did not know what to think. Mistress had been surprised that she had defended Minerva.

And Abigail did truly understand that Minerva had panicked.

But Minerva had also made a promise to Abigail. Abigail had not been asking for much, she thought. Just a public acknowledgment that she could sew a decent dress. "I would not see her punished."

"Do you need to see her again before you go?" Mistress asked the question gently.

But there was nothing gentle about the way pain sank into Abigail's chest.

No, Abigail would slip out of her life just as quietly as she slipped into it. She would content herself with the knowledge that she had taught Minerva almost as much as Minerva had taught her. Abigail could read now and Minerva understood who she was in a fundamentally different way. All told, it was an even enough exchange. "No. I don't think that's the best." It would put Minerva's reputation at risk and for what? Abigail was leaving. Immediately.

Mistress nodded and opened her mouth, as if she wanted to say something. She shut it, though, and turned her attention back to the papers before. Abigail took that as her sign to leave but before she could get the office door open, Mistress said, "She might come looking for you."

Here? "I don't think so." She couldn't imagine Minerva doing anything so bold as setting foot in the Jeweled Ladies. The risk was too great.

"All the same," Mistress said, "you might leave a letter for her. Just in case."

Just in case?

In case of what?

Chapter Seventeen

Abigail did not come to the schoolhouse on Sunday.

Minerva sat in the chair next to her stove, a blanket wrapped around her shoulders, and waited the entire night.

She waited in vain.

Nor did Abigail come to the Methodist Church Monday afternoon for their reading lesson. Minerva sat in the balcony of the church, watching the town go about its daily business through the small window.

She didn't see Abigail anywhere on the street. Not on Monday, not on Wednesday and not on Thursday.

She also did not see Abigail at the dry-goods store on Saturday. Minerva hadn't wanted to go back out in public. She didn't know what to wear. The too-fine dress that had started it all? The very nice skirt and jacket outfit? Or her old things? Her old, *ragged* things?

Minerva didn't feel right in any of it. She didn't want people to look at her in the too-fine dress. But she could not put on the old rags again, either.

In the end, she settled for the skirt and jacket. She tied the new bonnet onto her head and went out into the world.

As she marched down to the dry-goods store, she replayed for the millionth time what she would say to Abigail. She needed to apologize. She should've done so already but... How?

No, the best thing to do was to go about her regular errands and hope to run into Abigail. Maybe they would be able to have a few words. Maybe that would be long enough for Abigail to ask the girl to at least come to the schoolhouse tomorrow night so that she could apologize properly.

"Miss Krenshaw," Mrs. Snyder said in a frosty tone inside the dry-goods store.

Miranda took a step back. Was Mrs. Snyder mad at her? Then she remembered that it had been this woman who had first asked where she'd gotten such a nice dress. Had she been part of the trap? Or had she been just a curious bystander?

"Good day to you," she said, trying to smile and failing miserably. "I would like a..."

But Mrs. Snyder had moved off to help someone else. She had completely ignored a paying customer. Not that Minerva paid a lot, but she paid her bills.

She had been snubbed. There was no other word for it. Well, why wouldn't she be? The Snyders made a great deal of money selling fabrics and fripperies to the Jeweled Ladies.

Minerva looked around, hopeful to see Abigail or even Mistress. She could make her case to Mistress, if she had to. The store was busy, but she didn't see a single Jewel. At least, not until her gaze slid all the way back around and lit upon the woman that Mrs. Snyder had snubbed her for.

Mrs. Raymond Dupree—formerly Miss Emerald

Green, Mistress's prized Jewel—was making her weekly order.

Uncomfortable, Minerva scanned the store again. There was no one else. She could not loiter here all day long. Besides, the mayor's wife knew Abigail. Abigail had sewn dresses for this woman, both when she was a whore and now that she was a respectable woman. Or, at the very least, a respectable *enough* woman.

It would not harm Minerva's reputation to be seen talking to the mayor's wife.

Her resolve set, Minerva marched over to where Mrs. Dupree was waiting while Mrs. Snyder filled her order. "A word, Mrs. Dupree."

Mrs. Dupree did not look at her.

Minerva's chest began to tighten, as if a horse was sitting on her. "Mrs. Dupree?"

She knew that this woman could hear her. She could see the tight tension at her shoulders and the way her nostrils flared, as if Minerva had a particularly unpleasant odor today. But still, the mayor's wife did not acknowledge her.

Minerva quickly glanced around. No one was paying any attention to them and Mrs. Snyder was further behind the counter, weighing out sugar. "I need to speak to Abigail," she said in a whisper, trying to look casual about the entire situation. "Can you get a message to her for me?"

That got a reaction. Slowly, Mrs. Dupree swung her head around and tilted her chin up so that she could stare down her nose at Minerva. "I'm sorry."

"Abigail. Abigail Whithall?"

"Yes, I know Abigail. What I'm sorry about is

185

that you think I would help you." With that, she turned her face toward the counter and angled her head so that her wide hat blocked Minerva from view.

What? Minerva was being ignored. Completely. Which was…

Which was what she wanted, wasn't it? To be invisible and unseen? To know that people wouldn't look at her and ask questions of her?

"I need to apologize to her," Minerva whispered.

"It's a little late for that." She stepped around Minerva, moving closer to Mrs. Snyder.

Something about that statement struck her as wrong. Horribly, horribly wrong. "What's that supposed to mean?"

Mrs. Dupree swung around to face Minerva fully. She was still looking down her nose, even though they were of almost the same height. "Abigail is gone, Miss Krenshaw. She has taken her talents elsewhere, somewhere where she will be appreciated for her skills with the needle. Somewhere where she need not be ashamed of who she is." Mrs. Dupree leaned forward, her eyes narrowed with rage. "And for Abigail, clearly that place is not here. Good day." And once again, she turned her head so that the brim of her hat blocked Minerva from her sight.

The words were like blows to the body, making breathing impossible. Abigail had gone? She had just left Brimstone?

"Where did she go?" The question fell on deaf ears. Mrs. Snyder didn't look up at her and Mrs. Dupree didn't turn back to look at her and…

And she was invisible. Again.

Minerva looked around the store again. No one

noted her. No one was looking at the drape of her skirt or the cut of her jacket.

And Abigail had gone.

Minerva left the dry-goods store without really seeing where she was going. Somehow, she wound up back in the schoolroom. It was safe here, safe and respectable and *proper*. As long as she stayed in the schoolroom, alone, no one would ever know what went on in her heart or her head. Abigail was gone and no one would ever know that Minerva Krenshaw had been led into temptation by a beautiful girl who had loved her. Who Minerva had loved back.

She didn't realize she was crying until she went to scratch an itch on her cheek and discovered that it was wet. She should be happy. She was safe again. Abigail had gone and with her, Minerva's fear of exposure.

Minerva could stay in the schoolroom for the rest of her days, teaching generation after generation of children to read and do figures. Growing older and greyer and pricklier with each passing day. She would never leave the schoolhouse, never know warmth and laughter. There would only be approval and disapproval.

Abigail had gone without a word.

Did Minerva have any choice but to let her go?

*

She tried. She really did. Minerva tried her very best to put Abigail from her mind.

She spent a great deal of time at church. The Baptist Church, with its hard pews and hard rules, no longer felt like home.

187

A few times, she found herself in the balcony of the Methodist Church, watching the world walk by without her. No one noticed her coming and going. Why would they? She was just the schoolteacher.

She threw herself into a new round of raising funds for the school. New books. More chalk. The stable where some of the children tied their horses during the day—it needed to be repaired. She went to temperance meetings and lobbied business owners and...

She did everything she could to be seen and heard. To very little effect.

The sun still rose and set, although winter robbed the day of its light. Minerva spent more and more time sitting by the stove in the schoolroom, struggling to keep warm without using too much precious wood. But every night, as darkness filled the sky, misery would set in all over again because she could not help but think of the few glorious, wonderful times that Abigail had knocked on the schoolroom door after dark and spent hours in Minerva's arms.

She'd never gotten to apologize. That thought sat heavy on her. All she could see was the stunned, crumbling face of Abigail, right before Minerva had walked out of the dry-goods store. That face haunted her dreams, always just out of reach. Everywhere she went, Minerva saw reminders of Abigail.

She was miserable. And the thing was, she deserved it. It was all by her own doing. If she had only been able to resist the temptation of Abigail and her soft mouth and her warm body. But she hadn't. Minerva had sinned and now she was paying the penance. She would be doomed to be alone and miserable for the rest of her life

It was another Sunday night when she snapped. She simply could not take another night of sitting in that chair, then climbing into her freezing bed and trying not to think of Abigail. She couldn't *not* think about Abigail and it was making her miserable.

So she dressed. She put on the too-fine dress and then loosely tied on the skirt over that and then put her formerly best dress on over all of it. She wrapped on scarves and shawls and even threw a blanket over her head.

And then, before she could talk herself out of it, she headed down to town. She slipped down the alley behind the Jeweled Ladies because she couldn't bring herself to knock on the front door. There were lights on in the upper levels of the brothel, but the first floor was dark.

She knocked on the back door and waited. And waited. She knocked again, harder. There was no movement, no sign of life.

She was equally disappointed and relieved. This had been a foolish idea, anyway. She should just go back to the schoolhouse.

She turned to go but she hadn't gotten two feet when the door opened behind her. Startled, Minerva spun around.

A woman stood in the doorway—that wasn't surprising. She held a single candle up and peered at Minerva. Minerva was startled to realize that it was Mistress—but not the Mistress she was used to seeing out in public. There were no fancy gowns and no overbearing gems. Her hair hung in a loose braid over her shoulder and she was wrapped in a dressing gown.

Minerva knew that she needed to say something

189

or do something. She had come all this way to speak to this woman and plead for information about Abigail. To ask for help.

But it was just like the dry-goods store all over again. Her throat closed up and her mouth wouldn't work and she couldn't say what she needed to. So she just stood there like a bump on a log.

Mistress lowered the candle. "Took you long enough. Come on, before someone sees you."

And with that, she turned and was swallowed up by the darkness of the brothel.

Minerva hesitated a second before she followed Mistress into the dark room, which turned out to be a kitchen. Mistress shut the door behind her and threw the bolt and then silently, led her into the depths of the house. They started up the stairs, the light from the single candle throwing long shadows around them. They were halfway up when Mistress stopped. There were footsteps overhead, and the sound of a door shutting. Mistress waited a moment, and then continued up. And since Minerva was already here, she had no choice but to follow.

On the second floor, Mistress moved down the hallway toward the front of the house and into a surprisingly sparse room where an oil lamp burned on a desk. Mistress blew the candle out and sat behind the massive desk. "Close the door behind you, Miss Krenshaw."

Minerva did as she was told and then stood there, too nervous to know what to do next. It was hard not to stare at the woman behind the desk. It was harder to think of her as Mistress. Because right now, she did not look like a lady of the night. There was something about

190

her that was comfortable and relaxed—something that spoke to her age. She was not a young woman and right now, she was not a glamorous one, either.

"I'm sorry if I got you out of bed." It seemed the polite thing to say.

Mistress smirked. At least that hadn't changed, even though her lips were no longer painted a bright red. "You are not, but that's all right. I actually expected you much sooner. Coffee?" She motioned to an elaborate silver pot at the edge of the desk, where two china cups were balanced. One had coffee in it. "I was going over the books. Have a seat."

When Minerva didn't move right away, Mistress studied her. "Do you need to remove your clothing?"

"No!" Minerva said, clutching her chest. That was when she remembered she had on more clothing than normal. She unwound herself from the blanket and folded it over her arm. "I mean, I'm quite comfortable. Thank you."

Mistress smirked again. Minerva did not care for it. "Suit yourself. How may I help you this evening, Miss Krenshaw?"

All of the things Minerva had wanted to say seemed to abandon her in her time of need. "Do you know where Abigail is?"

Mistress dropped her gaze to the desk, tracing a well-manicured finger over the ledger sheet, as if she were uninterested in this conversation. "Of course I do."

Minerva swallowed and took a step deeper into the room. "Will you tell me where she is?"

"I will not." It was said in such a matter of fact way, as if Minerva had asked to borrow five dollars instead of asking for Abigail's whereabouts.

The pain in her chest was crushing. It made her want to double over. If Mistress wouldn't help her and the mayor's wife wouldn't help her—then no one would. No one else would know where Abigail was and Minerva would have to spend the rest of her life reliving this great mistake over and over again.

"Is she—is she well?"

Mistress looked up from her ledgers, shadows deep on her face. Maybe it wasn't shadows. Maybe it was just age that was no longer hidden under thick makeup. "If you don't mind me asking, Miss Krenshaw, why do you care?"

And Minerva was forced to deal with the realization that, outside of Abigail, Mistress was the only other person who *knew*. Or at least, who surmised what the truth of her and Abigail's relationship had really been.

And Abigail had promised Mistress would never reveal her secrets, or any of the other secrets she held over nearly every person in this town.

She knew what she needed to do, what she needed to say. Now if she could only make herself actually say it.

Mistress waited for a moment and then, exhaling heavily, she returned her attention back to the ledger. Minerva felt the dismissal, one she'd earned.

"I love her," she blurted out.

If she'd shocked Mistress, the other woman didn't show it. "You have a rather odd way of showing it."

That was probably a generous way to put it. "I love her but I don't know *how* to love her."

Mistress sat back and looked up at the ceiling. "She defended you, you know. She sat in this chair,"

192

she said, gesturing to a chair in front of the desk, "and defended you to me. She understood that you panicked. She wasn't surprised that you couldn't do it, not with everyone watching. She made me promise not to come after you for using her wrong." Mistress kept her voice light, but there was no missing that threat.

A shiver went down Minerva's back. "Why didn't you?"

"Because," Mistress said, glancing up at her through her lashes. "I gave my word and although it may not mean much to you, I honor my word. I protect my own." There was a long pause before Mistress added quietly, "And that does not include you."

Minerva had never been beaten. Her parents had been kind and compassionate to both their only child and the runaways who came looking for help. She had never been attacked or assaulted. She had never had to endure the level of pain and humiliation that Abigail and too many women like her had.

But Mistress's words hit her like blows anyway, robbing her of breath and sending pain spiking through her body. This time, she did double over, her arms wrapped around her waist. "I just wanted to tell her I was sorry," she said, which was when she realized she was sobbing. If pride went before a fall, she had fallen completely. "I didn't get to tell her I was sorry before she left. I kept hoping that she might come and see me or that I would see her on the street and then Mrs. Dupree said she was gone already and I didn't get to tell her."

If she expected comfort from Mistress, she was wrong. "Abigail put her faith in you, Minerva. She came alive because of you. I nursed her back to health and it's true, I gave her a devil's bargain. Work on her

193

back for me and she'd get that shop that she wanted. It was the best way for her to get the money and she did it. But she never really lost that dead look in her eyes while she worked for me. Not until you. You set her free in a way that I couldn't. She trusted you. And in the end, what did you do?"

Minerva's knees gave as she crumpled to the floor, keening. She deserved this, she deserved it all—but that didn't mean it hurt any less.

"Yet..." Mistress said, her voice penetrating through Minerva's cries. "And yet she sat here and defended you anyway. Do you know why? Because she loves you, too. Foolish girl that she is, to give her heart to someone who did not prove worthy. But then, we've all made that mistake before, haven't we?"

She had. She had kissed Eliza and regretted it for ten long years. She had regretted losing her reputation and her family and her community but she hadn't had a choice. She couldn't stay in New York and live in fear that Eliza would shred her reputation when she'd least expect it.

She couldn't have stayed there and forced herself to marry out of a sense of duty. As much as she missed her home and her family, she couldn't have been who she was if she had stayed in New York.

And Abigail couldn't be who she was if she stayed in Brimstone. With Minerva.

She didn't know how much time passed. Eventually, she managed to get herself under control and at least sit up so that she wasn't a pitiful, helpless heap of clothing on the floor. When she did so, she found that Mistress was watching her closely. "You won't help me?"

Mistress shook her head slowly. "Aside from the fact that it is not my place to tell you where Abigail has gone to, you must look at the reality of the situation, Minerva. You have a place in this town—a place you value greatly. Winter is upon us and, if I'm not mistaken, you have a contractual obligation to continue teaching for the next five months. Even if I provided you her whereabouts, there's nothing you can do about it without wandering off into a blizzard in the mountains and dying of frostbite or starvation—or worse."

It was a surprisingly logical statement, but logic didn't make it any better. She pulled herself to her feet and tried to speak around the tightness in her throat. "I understand. If you… If you send her a letter, would you tell her that I'm sorry? That I never meant to hurt her and that I miss her dearly?"

Mistress regarded her for a long moment. "I will think about it." She turned her attention back to her ledgers.

That was it. Her fate rested entirely upon a woman who did not like her and did not respect her. Not that Minerva had done anything to earn that respect. She hadn't.

She was at the door when Mistress spoke again. "There's a basket there—yes, that one. She left that for you."

Minerva turned around and gaped at the woman, but she wasn't paying any attention. All of Mistress's attention was focused on that ledger.

There was a small basket right by the door. Minerva picked it up.

"Go out the way you came. And be sure to shut the door," Mistress said behind her.

Minerva wrapped the blanket around her head and tucked the basket into the crook of her arm.

And then she closed the door behind her.

It was a skirt and a shirt. The shirt was unfinished, the hems undone and the fabric more billowy than the other shirt she had. Minerva was reasonably sure that Abigail had been planning on adding more seams. But if she tucked it in, it wouldn't matter. And unlike the navy blue skirt and jacket, the skirt was a rich, russet brown. Minerva wouldn't have thought the color brown could be pretty but then, it seemed everything Abigail touched could be made pretty.

Even her.

At the bottom of the basket was a folded piece of paper. Minerva sat looking at it for a long time, letting herself cry. Even as Abigail had walked away from her, she had left Minerva with these gifts. She had cared enough not to take the clothing with her. Minerva couldn't help but feel that Abigail, wherever she was, still wanted Minerva to wear them.

Finally, she pulled the paper out of the basket and angled it toward the dying firelight.

Thank you for teaching me to read and write. I shall keep practicing. I will not waste your gift. Sincerely, Abigail Whithall.

The handwriting was neat and legible. Everything was spelled correctly. The sentences were well constructed.

The rejection was complete.

Minerva cried into the skirt that still smelled faintly of lavender. Of Abigail.

She had no one to blame but herself.

Chapter Eighteen

The winter was dark and dreary. Minerva went through the motions of teaching. She lost even more weight, which made Abigail's clothes fit her poorly again. It was difficult to care, though. This was the rest of her life.

It was February when the note was delivered. Megan Snyder came up to her just before class began and handed Minerva a cream envelope, scented with lilacs. "Mama says I'm to give this to you," the youngest Snyder child said.

Minerva stared down at the envelope. The paper was heavy and the edge of the envelope was scalloped. This was expensive stuff. There was no name on the envelope, no handwriting at all. "Is it from your mother?"

Little Megan shook her head. "The fancy lady gave it to her."

The...*fancy* lady? But Minerva knew better than to ask any other questions because the other children were filing in and taking their seats and it was time for the lessons to begin and she didn't want to draw attention to the fact that she had gotten an anonymous letter. So she tucked it inside her desk drawer and went about her day. For the first time in a long time, however, she felt a pang of anticipation. Because who else could the letter be from if not the fanciest of fancy ladies in this town, Mistress? Who else would own such expensive stationery and such expensive perfume?

Had Mistress heard from Abigail? Oh, she dearly hoped so. Be good news, she prayed. Surely, if it were bad news, Mistress would not break it to her in a letter.

Would she?

If Minerva thought the previous few months had passed slowly, they had nothing on this particular day. She didn't dare read the letter during the lunch break. She couldn't risk having a student interrupt her or—depending on the news—be so upset that she couldn't continue with the afternoon's lessons. So the letter sat unread until the last of the students had headed down the hill and back to their families.

Minerva gave it an additional fifteen minutes, during which she frantically straightened up the schoolroom. As if the letter signified a visitor. *Ha.* She really had lost her mind.

Finally, she couldn't take another moment of waiting. She shot the bolt on the door and all but ran to the desk. With shaking hands, she broke the seal on the letter and lifted the scalloped edge away. There was a single sheet of paper inside and the script was elaborate and flowing.

It was not Abigail's hand. It was not Abigail's scent.

The wave of disappointment broke over her, but she pushed it aside and focused on the letter.

Miss Krenshaw, I've had a letter from Abigail. She is well and settling into her new shop. The fabrics she ordered from San Francisco have arrived and she's building up a steady clientele of both respectable women and ladies such as myself. She asked after you. What shall I tell her? M

Up until the moment she had learned that Abigail had left Brimstone, Minerva had never been a crier. Tears were wasted emotion and that energy could be better spent on solving problems. She had always faced the future with firm resolve and dedication to the task in front of her.

But as she held Mistress's letter, Minerva let herself cry. These were not tears of pain, although there was pain. They were tears of relief. Abigail was well. She had her shop. Ladies were paying her to make dresses.

Abigail had asked after her.

There were a few clues in the short note. Abigail had told Minerva all those months ago that she was considering going to San Francisco or maybe Virginia City. If she had ordered fabrics from San Francisco, that meant she was not there. Was she in Virginia City? Or had she settled somewhere else? Denver? There were a lot of boomtowns around gold and silver mines, but most of them were not big enough to have respectable ladies of means.

Minerva had a map on the wall of her schoolroom, one of the country that spanned from ocean to ocean. Virginia City was in Nevada and Minerva was in Texas. It was at least fifteen hundred miles from Brimstone to Virginia City. There were wide swaths of hostile territories between the two towns, not to mention several mountain ranges. Mountain ranges that were probably still buried in snowed and would remain so for months more.

She remembered Mistress's warning. Travel in the winter would be nearly impossible.

And that didn't even take into account the biggest roadblock—how was she to pay her way? She couldn't very well walk to Nevada.

As Minerva did not have fine stationery—or, for that matter, any stationary at all—she carefully unfolded the envelope and wrote her reply directly on the inside of it.

Madam, words cannot express my gratitude to receive your note.

Minerva sat and stared at the first line for a while. If she had paper to spare, she would consider crossing it out and starting over. How exactly did one write this sort of letter? What was she to say?

Please tell Abigail that I continue on. I wear the skirts and shirts and jackets daily and I wear the fine dress to church on Sundays. I cut up my old dresses to make a winter cloak and I do not wear them otherwise. I would hope that she would be pleased to hear that. Please tell her that I miss her terribly and that I'm sorry I never got to apologize to her. For I remain sorry for hurting her to this day and I shall for the rest of my days. Please tell her that I love her and I always will and I would give anything to be able to make it up to her. Please tell her I wish nothing but the best for her and her happiness will evermore be mine.

Minerva stared at the words for a while, feeling shaken by the truth of them. Perhaps she ought not to have committed such honest sentiments to the page. Perhaps she ought not to entrust this letter to Mistress, as it was proof of her fall into temptation and sin. Proof she had fallen in love.

She folded the envelope back onto itself, but lacked any wax or glue that would hold it shut. Well. This would not do. She could not very well give an unsealed letter to Megan Snyder, nor could she give such an unsealed letter to Mrs. Snyder. That would be the quickest way for her business to become common knowledge. It was bad enough that Mistress knew everything. Minerva could not have the townsfolk know anything.

So she did the only thing she could think of. She put on her straw bonnet, tucked the envelope into a pocket, and went to town.

*

The bell over her door chimed and Janie Bradford moved farther back behind the screen. "Who is it?" she whispered, clutching the green muslin to her chest.

Abigail straightened just as Hubert, Janie's man, called out, "Is my Janie in here?"

Smirking, Abigail looked up at Janie, who visibly relaxed. "I'm here, baby," the older woman called back. "But you can't look just yet."

"Dang it all," Hubert grumbled, winking at Abigail. "I've got deliveries for you, hon—looks like more fabric. Oh, and a letter came for you," he added, laying it on the counter.

"Thanks, Hubert. Do you mind stacking the bolts for me?"

This was a normal day in Virginia City—well, normal enough. Janie was always nervous about being caught in the dress store. She maintained that a black woman was bad for Abigail's business, but Abigail steadfastly maintained that was nonsense. She'd dressed women of color and Indian women and the finest white ladies in the state of Nevada. Janie had been one of her first customers because the other dressmakers in town wouldn't dress a mixed-race woman. Hubert was a jack-of-all-trades and Janie ran a boarding house that catered to black people.

Although Hubert was white and he and Janie couldn't marry, they'd helped introduce her into the colored community here. Between that and the support of several madams who were greatly pleased with Abigail's dresses, it had only taken six months, for White's to be established as *the* place to go for the latest dresses.

Really, this was everything she had ever wanted. She had a nice shop in a nice part of town. She had as much work as she could want. There were a great many brothels in Virginia City and all of the ladies wanted to look their best. But there were also women like Janie Bradford, whose menfolk had silver money. They all wanted nice things.

The back of the shop held a cozy set of rooms with comfortable furniture that was hers. She spent her nights with silks and satins instead of gentlemen callers.

Indeed, it was almost perfect.

Almost.

She finished pinning Janie's dress and then went to read her letter while the woman changed. "I've got cookies for when you're done," she told Hubert as he made another trip in. Abigail was selling so many dresses so quickly that she couldn't keep her stock up. Hubert delivered more fabric every week.

"Those winds are strong again. Anything not tied down is about to be blown off the side of this mountain," he said as he loaded the bolts into racks Abigail had built along the walls.

Abigail made noises of sympathy as she went back behind the desk and opened the letter from Mistress.

Abigail, I'm ever pleased when I receive a letter from you. Your handwriting improves all the time and it does me proud. Enclosed is a note from Minerva.

Suddenly, her hands were shaking. There was more to the letter, but Abigail put that aside because a piece of paper in a different hand fell out of the envelope.

Please tell Abigail that I continue on. I wear the skirts and shirts and jackets daily and I wear the fine dress to church on Sundays.

Abigail blinked tears as she read the message.

Please tell her that I love her.

"You all right?" Abigail looked up to find Janie standing in front of her, worry on her kind features.

Abigail sniffed and swiped at her cheeks with the back of her hand. "Oh, I'm fine. Just a letter from a…from an old friend. I miss her dearly."

Janie mulled this over. "Any chance she can visit you?"

Abigail tried to shrug, as if everything were fine when it wasn't. Because there was one thing missing from her life here. She had safety and security. She had her shop and enough money in the bank that she would never go hungry. She had friends and customers and no one was in control of her life. Except for her.

Indeed, there was only one thing missing.

Please tell her I love her and I always will.

"Probably not." Because if Minerva came to visit, Abigail might not let her leave. She'd want to share her bed not just once a week, but every night. She'd want to have the kind of closeness that Hubert and Janie Bradford got to have all the time. Although they couldn't marry, either, Hubert was officially a boarder at Janie's house and they were able to be together.

Obviously, she and Minerva wouldn't announce to the world that they were in love. Abigail wasn't stupid. They would do what any number of women in this town did—share a house to save money, because it was safer than being a woman alone.

But she just didn't think Minerva could do that. She would be forever worried about what people might say or think or accidentally see. Minerva might spend the rest of their lives worrying about her reputation instead of living her life. And as much as Abigail wanted her, she didn't want to spend the rest of her life having to make choices based on what other people thought was proper. This was her new start, her fresh beginning. She made her own choices for her own reasons. Not for anyone else.

Sadly, not even for Minerva.

"It can be lonely out here," Janie said softly. "About broke my heart when Hubert left me in Virginia to stake his claim. I thought I might never see him again."

Abigail looked up at her friend in confusion. Every time she had seen the two of them together, Hubert and Janie acted like a pair of lovebirds. Nothing could keep them apart—could it? "What happened?"

Janie shrugged, looking sheepish. "He felt he had to prove he could be the man who took care of me. After he made enough money, he wrote and asked me to come. I almost didn't."

"Why not? He loves you."

"Honey," Janie said and suddenly Abigail felt very young. What would her life have been like if someone like Janie and Hubert had been her parents? "I'm black—and a former slave. My momma was a slave and my daddy owned her. I love my man dearly but we can't marry or have children. I thought that, if I let him go, he'd eventually see the light and find a proper girl to marry. But he wouldn't give up and I couldn't fight what we've got. He hired a woman to teach me to read. He bought the boarding house to make sure I'd have a place, you know? It's in my name. No matter what happens, it's mine. He made sure that I would never be at anyone's mercy ever again. That's when I realized he'd never let me go and I'd never find a better man. What man, black or white, would do that for someone like *me*?"

Abigail ducked her head. No doubt, Hubert and Janie had guessed enough of the truth. "I didn't know you'd been a slave. I…I know what that's like."

Janie looked at her kindly and patted her on the cheek. "You're a sweet girl, Abigail. Almost like the daughter we never had. It's not always easy for people like us, but it gets better."

Abigail looked around her shop. Hubert was lingering near the front door, cookies in hand. She got the feeling he was standing guard so she and Janie could have this talk. "It's already better. This shop— it's everything I ever wanted."

Janie nodded. "But there's more to life than a livelihood, isn't there? Lots of people don't think Hubert and I should be together. Lord knows it's not legal. But we don't care about that. I just needed to have more faith in him and he needed to have more faith in me."

Faith? Abigail stared at Minerva's note. Had she realized that Mistress would include the whole thing? She must not have. The letter was addressed to Mistress entirely.

"You come out for dinner tonight, you hear? I've got a new cook for the dining room." Abigail looked back up at her friend, her brown eyes smiling and her face worried. "We need you to test her biscuits."

"I will," she promised.

Janie patted her cheek again and headed for the door. But before she left, she turned back and said, "Don't give up on your friend. If she's writing you, she hasn't given up on you, either."

After the Bradfords were gone, Abigail read the letter again and again. She had been so upset when Minerva had panicked and walked out of the dry-goods store that it had seemed like leaving was the only way to move forward.

She hadn't given Minerva a chance to apologize. She hadn't given her a chance to make it up to her. At the time it seemed like a clean break would be best. It was time to leave Ebony White behind. Abigail had also left behind Abigail Whithall. Instead, when she arrived in Virginia City, she had forged a new identity, one that was all parts of her past. She'd gotten rid of Mrs. Whithall's last name. The woman had never deserved the honor of being Abigail's namesake. But she hadn't been Ebony anymore either.

Abigail White had felt right.

After all this time, Minerva still wrote this letter. She still spoke of true happiness and love. The note wasn't bitter or even polite. Minerva had written this letter to Mistress and poured her heart out, probably knowing full well that it was a risk to her reputation.

And the truth was, Abigail missed her. Minerva's absence was so deep that it almost felt like an additional person living in the shop with her. She missed Mistress and she missed her friends among the Jewels. But she didn't lay awake in bed at night, tormented with longing for *them*. She didn't miss the brothel and she certainly didn't miss the men. She hadn't slept with a single person in months. Her body was her own now and it longed for only one person.

Minerva.

Maybe nothing would come of this, she thought as she pulled out a fresh sheet of paper—another luxury—and started writing. She had to write two copies of every letter—the first just to get the words on the page. Then she would go back and check her spelling and make sure that she had used the right word at the right time. Then she would carefully recopy the letter in her best handwriting. It took time, but it was worth it.

It was time to figure out if she was worth the risk.

Chapter Nineteen

Minerva pounded on the back door of the brothel. The sun had barely set and a few stragglers had probably seen her on her way here, but she did not care. The fact that she had managed to wait until Sunday evening was a miracle in itself.

She held the letter from Abigail in her hand. The one addressed to *her*, not to Mistress. The one where Abigail told Minerva how much she missed her, how much she wished they'd had more time together. How much she loved her little shop in Virginia City, and how even though she had made friends, she was so lonely.

The letter where Abigail had, it seemed to Minerva, said everything around *come to me* without actually saying it.

She banged on the door some more.

Because if Abigail were going to forgive her, Minerva wanted to hear it from her own lips. Not from a letter, not from a message sent through Mistress. She wanted to look Abigail in the eyes and hear her say the words and then Minerva wanted to say her own words. Words like *love* and *honor* and *respect*. Words like *forever* and *together*.

Seventeen hundred miles was nothing. She would walk it if she had to.

After what felt like a very long time, the back door to the brothel was thrown open. It had been a month since Minerva had found Mistress at the baker's and thrust the unsealed envelope into her hands. Since then, she had not seen this woman at all.

Mistress was once again in that dressing gown, her face relatively free of paint. But instead of looking annoyed, she seemed almost pleased to see Minerva. "Well, come in."

Silently, the two women tromped up to Mistress's office. Minerva didn't hesitate—she walked over and sat in the chair in front of the desk. "I had a letter from Abigail."

"Did you?" Mistress did not sound surprised by this. Indeed, she didn't even seem excited. All of her attention was on the ledger books in front of her. At least that hadn't changed. "It is good to see that she is using her education to become a fine correspondent."

"I think she might be willing to forgive me."

"Is that so." It was not a question. It was barely polite conversation.

"Yes. But there's a problem."

Still, Mistress did not look up from her books. "Is there?"

Minerva got the distinct feeling that Mistress was toying with her as a cat might toy with a terrified mouse. Except Minerva wasn't a little mouse anymore. She wasn't going to hide from the one thing she wanted, the one thing that made her who she was. She'd spent ten years denying who she was. And that time was over. "Yes. I don't have the money to go to Virginia City."

"No, I imagine the poor schoolmistress would

209

not. But I fail to see what that has to do with me." She turned the page in her ledger.

Minerva took a deep breath. "I'd like a loan. To buy a ticket on a coach."

That got Mistress's attention. She glanced up at Minerva and then burst out into a laugh. "You would, would you? I don't recall hanging out a shingle announcing that I was open for banking business, Miss Krenshaw."

"I'll pay you back."

"With what money? You have nothing, my dear woman. Even the clothes on your back—those came from me, whether you like to admit it or not. You have nothing to give me, nothing in exchange that I would find valuable."

It wasn't unexpected, that argument. "You care for her. I wouldn't have thought it possible, but you do. She told me how you saved her. You engaged me to teach her to read because you wanted her to succeed." Mistress did not deny this, so Minerva continued. "I don't think you like it that she's out there by herself. I think it bothers you that she is unprotected and alone. I think you worry about her and I think that you would feel better if you knew that I was with her."

"So you can hurt her again? There's a flaw in your argument, Miss Krenshaw."

Heat rose in Minerva's cheeks, but she ignored the blush. "And let us not forget you don't like me. You never have. This is your chance to get rid of me. My teaching contract will be up soon. I could leave and never come back and when you think of me it would only be to know that I was spending the rest of my life making sure Abigail was happy and well."

Mistress laughed again. Somehow, it seemed more honest. "You are indeed the most prickly woman I have ever known, Miss Krenshaw. Sometimes I wonder what that girl sees in you."

Minerva thought back to the letter, printed in Abigail's own hand. Her writing was getting stronger, she could tell. The strokes of the letters were more sure and the spelling was perfect. "It is because I see her as she is, not as I wish her to be. And the thing that amazes me all the more is that I think she sees me, too. Prickliness and all."

Surprisingly, Mistress did not laugh at that. One corner of her mouth curved up into a smile. "She gave you her address, did she?

Minerva shook her head. "She said she was in Virginia City. Even in a town growing as fast as that one surely is, there cannot be that many colored seamstresses named Abigail Whithall who own a dress shop. I would not risk such a journey only to be deterred by a small detail as a precise address."

She would, however, be deterred by a lack of funds. She really did not want to walk across Comanche territory. She would prefer not to die in a desert or stranded in a mountain pass.

After all, this was not exactly the kind of thing that the First Macon County Bank gave out loans for. Mr. Hobbs would laugh her out of the bank and probably out of town.

If this didn't work, Minerva had one other option. Free Cyrus Franklin, the freeman who lived outside of town. He was rumored to help runaways and other people in distress on their way west. He had gotten a great deal of money from somewhere, people said.

211

There had been various rumors about where, exactly, that money had come from, but they were unproven.

He might be willing to help her. But then she would have to explain why it was so important that she get to Abigail and she did not know the man nearly well enough to guess whether or not true love between two women would move him to part with his money.

Not that Mistress was motivated by true love, either. But Minerva was right—the woman did care for Abigail in her own way.

So she sat. Mistress let her sit. Long minutes stretched as the two women waited to see which one would break first. After a while, Minerva began to doubt that Mistress would help her. Perhaps she had misjudged the madam. Perhaps the happiness of a former Jewel was no longer a concern of hers.

But just when Minerva truly began to despair, Mistress sighed heavily, marking her place in the ledger with a finger. "I don't know how you think you're going to pay me back. What are you going to do in Virginia City, get another teaching position? It's true they may pay slightly more than they do here, but I doubt that's enough to cover a coach fare or a guide to accompany and protect you. You are correct in that I do not care for you but I am loath to send a fellow woman to a near-certain death."

Minerva smiled. "Recently, I was hired to do some tutoring outside of the schoolroom. I am quite sure that there are some newly wealthy gentlemen in Virginia City who could do with improving their letters and diction." When Mistress didn't reply immediately, Minerva added, "And if I leave, they'll have to hire a new teacher. Perhaps you could have a say in the matter—indirectly, of course."

Mistress looked like she was biting her inner cheek to keep from smiling. "It's true that I would pay a great deal of money to never speak to you again."

Minerva couldn't even be insulted by that statement—she was too excited by the promise of help that lurked underneath the barb. "How much money?"

Mistress lost her fight against the smile. She leaned back in her chair and stared up at the ceiling, once again appealing to heaven above. "God save me from women in love. If I do this for you—you will understand that I'm not actually doing it for you at all. I'm doing it for Abigail. Part of the deal will be reminding Abigail to write me regularly. I do enjoy knowing that she is well."

Minerva had won. More than that, she had received what amounted to Mistress's blessing. Abigail had no one else that qualified as family.

She was going to leave Brimstone. The thought was terrifying and exciting and excitingly terrifying all at once. She was going to make a long, dangerous journey and at the end, she prayed she would find forgiveness and hope and a future, although those things were not guaranteed. But her only other choice was to stay here in Brimstone and slowly waste away, living only half of her life and never again tasting happiness.

She lifted her chin and smiled. "Of course, Mistress."

Mistress pulled out a sheet of paper and wrote on it before handing it over to Minerva. It was a bank draft for two hundred and fifty dollars—more money than Minerva had in two years. "Then we have a deal. Goodbye, Miss Krenshaw."

Minerva took the bank draft and stood. "Goodbye, Mistress. I wish you well."

Mistress nodded her head in acknowledgment and turned her attention back to the ledger. Minerva had reached the door before she spoke again. "Oh, Miss Krenshaw?"

"Yes?"

"She doesn't go by Whithall anymore. She decided to do away with her former owner's name. She goes by White now. Abigail White."

For some reason, that made Minerva smiled. "That is a perfect name for her. Thank you, Mistress."

Then she walked out of the office and away from the Jeweled Ladies for the last time.

On Monday, she would inform Mayor Dupree that she would not be renewing her teaching contract.

And then she would begin to make her plans.

Chapter Twenty

Spring in Virginia City was different from spring in Brimstone. Brimstone was dry and windy, but the wind here was something else entirely. It would tear doors off hinges if a person didn't approach it with the proper respect. Abigail found that she had to design her hats and skirts differently, lest her customers be caught unawares and exposed.

She went to church with the Bradfords and took meals with them once or twice a week. She made friends with several of the doves who worked at the various saloons and brothels. She didn't tell people that she'd been a whore, but some of the girls figured it out anyway. The Jeweled Ladies had been one of the richest brothels in Texas but it had nothing on even the most everyday brothel here in Virginia City. Silver flowed out of the mountains and into the girls' hands faster than any of them could count.

Abigail, however, counted. While she enjoyed small indulgences, like all the paper she wanted to write on and books and newspapers to read, she did not spend wildly. There would come a time when Virginia City ran out of silver. Having money in the bank was always a good backup plan.

The days passed quickly enough. She met with

customers and sewed dresses and joked with Hubert and Janie. But every day, she watched the door for the mail. It had been almost three months since she had written a letter to Minerva. She couldn't imagine Minerva *not* writing a response. True, she hadn't exactly given her precise address to Minerva. But Mistress knew how to reach her and Minerva had already demonstrated a willingness to talk to Mistress.

Any day now, a letter would come. She knew it, deep in her heart.

It was late in the afternoon when she heard the bell over the door chime. Abigail said, "I'll be right with you," as she finished sliding the last bolt of fabric back onto the rack. Next time, she would order a different shade of red silk. Something that was unexpected. The girls would be fighting over it, she thought with a smile.

Mental note made, she turned back to her newest customer. The afternoon sunlight slanted in to the store windows, hiding the two people who stood just inside her shop deep in shadows. But it was a man and a woman, that she could see clearly. And not Hubert and Janie. The woman was too tall and thin. Too pale. "Can I help you?"

"This is the right place?" The man asked in a rough voice.

"It is."

Everything about Abigail came to a sudden halt. *Was that…*

But before her brain could make sense of that voice, the woman turned to the man and said, "Thank you very much, Gilbert. I shall be sure to tell Mistress that you discharged your duties with honor."

216

The man—Gilbert—touched his fingers to the brim of his worn hat. "Much obliged, ma'am." The man nodded in Abigail's direction and then he was back out the door, the bell ringing to mark his exit.

She had come. Minerva Krenshaw herself was standing inside Abigail's dress shop.

After a long moment, Minerva stepped forward and untied her bonnet—the bonnet Abigail had gotten her—and pulled it from her head. Abigail saw as she came deeper into the shop that Minerva was wearing the royal blue dress—the one that she had been so uncomfortable in all of those months ago. As she set the bonnet down on the counter and took another step toward Abigail, she couldn't help but think that Minerva didn't look uncomfortable in it at all.

They just stared at each other for a long moment while Abigail tried to figure out if her heart was going to beat clean free of her chest or not. Finally, she couldn't stand it anymore. "You're here."

"I got your letter. I wanted to respond in person."

Abigail knew her mouth was open to her chest but she couldn't stop staring. "You came all this way instead of just writing me a letter?" Her head spun, so she clutched at the end of the counter for support.

Minerva opened her mouth and then closed it and then took another step into the shop. Only about six feet—the length of the counter—separated them now and Abigail could see that Minerva's face was drawn and she had lost even more weight. She looked very much like a woman who had suffered through a long, lonely winter.

But Abigail could also now see something else— she could see Minerva's eyes. They didn't look haunted and sad. There was a light to them that sparked hope in her chest. Which was foolish because where had hope ever gotten her before?

No, she would not get her hopes up. Just because Minerva had made the journey of approximately seventeen hundred miles did not mean there was any reason to hope.

"I apologize, Abigail. I made you a promise and I did not uphold that promise. I hurt your feelings and, in not giving you credit for your work, I diminished you in the eyes of the people around us. I have no excuse. Mistress has told me that you defended me, even after I betrayed you. It was not necessary to do so. I deserved no such protections from you."

In all the nights that Abigail had lain awake in her bed in the back room of this shop, imagining what it would be like if Minerva were to suddenly and unexpectedly appear before her, she had never imagined it going quite like this. Maybe that was because no one had ever apologized to her before. Not Mrs. Whithall. Even Mistress had not apologized for neglecting to teach Abigail to read.

Abigail had never been worthy of an apology before.

She saw Minerva swallow nervously. "I understand if you cannot forgive me for that. I was the one person whom you should have been able to count on. I promise you that I will not fail you again."

"Why are you here?" Abigail asked breathlessly because she didn't want this to be a misunderstanding. She didn't want to risk her heart again only to hear Minerva say that she was just passing through on her way to San Francisco.

Minerva straightened, a shadow falling over her face. "I did not renew my teaching contract in Brimstone. I borrowed the money to get this far. I came to apologize, but I have no intention of going back." She reached over and picked up her bonnet, nervously threading the ribbon through her fingers. "I came to apologize," she repeated, sounding as if she were schooling a student. But then she softened, adding, "But..."

"But?" Because that was certainly the most important word in the whole of the English language. Everything rested upon that one word.

Minerva looked down to where she had knotted the ribbon around her fingers. "But I came to start over. I have no right to ask you to give me another chance, but I cannot imagine ever being happy again without you next to me. It doesn't matter what your name is or was—you will always be Abigail to me and that is all that I want. Just you."

And, dammit, hope broke free from the little wall she had built around it in her heart. All of the things Abigail wanted and never allowed herself to truly dream of having—they were all right there. Right in front of her, waiting for her answer.

"You made a promise to me," she said softly. "You would tell people that I made your dresses so they would see that I could sew a respectable dress."

Minerva's cheeks colored. "I know. I didn't just let you down. I let myself down, as well. I always thought that I was this person who was above sin and temptation. If I could just do everything right, I would *be* right. I took a perverse sort of pride in being poorly dressed, in being poor. I convinced myself that if I kept clear of temptation, what I knew was true in my heart wouldn't be wrong. And then I met you and everything I thought I knew was proven wrong over and over again. Because the truth is that the woman I thought I was is a fraction of who I am. It's only when I was with you that I could see a different life. And I couldn't face it then."

Abigail's heart really was going to explode, it was beating so hard and fast. "Now?"

She shrugged, a little smile gracing her perfect lips. "Sometimes, if you want to start over, you have to go someplace new. No one knows me here. No one will look at me and think, 'there's that prickly Miss Krenshaw, the prim schoolmarm who has no friends and will forever be alone.' Here, I can be someone else."

"You're not going to be a prickly schoolmarm anymore?" But even as she asked the question, Abigail began to smile.

"Oh, I'll still be the prickly schoolmarm. There are some things that will never change. But now, when someone asks me where I get my dresses, I'm going to tell them the truth. Now, when people see me on the street, they'll think, 'there goes prickly Miss Krenshaw. I don't know how that lovely Miss White can stand to be friends with her.'" Her smile faded. "That is, if you still want to be friends with me. More than friends."

"Lovers?"

In Brimstone, if Abigail had said that word out loud, Miranda might've fainted dead away.

But now? She didn't even look wounded by the word. Instead, her whole face lit up and Abigail saw hope reflected back at her. It was the look of happiness. "Lovers. More than lovers. I want to grow old with you—never mind that I am already old."

"I don't think of you that way, you know."

Minerva took a step toward and Abigail realized that she was doing the same. "And I don't think of you as too young. I love you, Abigail. I have loved you since the very first and my great regret in life is that I did not show it properly before. But if you'll give me the chance, I will spend the rest of my days by your side, loving you for as long as we both live."

Everything about her wanted to throw herself in Minerva's arms and hold her tight. But she didn't. Not yet. There'd already been too much unspoken between them once. She wouldn't let it happen again. "I won't have you be ashamed of me. I can't change anything about my life in the past. I'll always be a former slave. I'll always have horrible memories. I'll always have a little bit of Ebony White in me. I even took that name here, you know."

Minerva was close enough to touch. She reached out and cupped Abigail's cheek. "I know. It's perfect for you because it's who you became to save yourself. I wasn't ashamed of you back in Brimstone. I was ashamed of myself. I couldn't figure out how to be the spinster schoolteacher and also a woman who loves you, and I made the wrong choice."

"You did," Abigail said, but she was smiling too much now, her eyes pricking with happy tears.

"I would spare you the suffering of your past if I could, but I do not think less of you as a person for it. I will never be ashamed of you. The only thing I can do is promise you that in the future, I will honor your wishes and support your choices. Even if you choose for me not to be a part of your life." Her eyes shone at this last bit as her thumb stroked over Abigail's cheek. "Will you have me? The choice is yours."

Abigail did wrap her arms around Minerva then, stepping in close and breathing in the scent of her—lye soap and a hint of that tartness—plus dust. Lots of dust. "You came here first, didn't you?"

Minerva rested her lips against Abigail's forehead. "We had to stop and ask around. There's only one White's, though. The only reason I didn't come sooner was because it was winter." She leaned back and looked down at Abigail. "I would have come no matter what. I would have walked here, if I had to. I have faith in you, Abigail. I know you're going to do wonderful things—sew wonderful dresses—without me. You don't need my seal of respectability here. But I hope that you want me. Because I want you."

"I shouldn't have run," she said, burying her face in Minerva's shoulder. Janie's words about having faith came back to her. "I should have at least stayed in Brimstone long enough to see you one more time. I left you without a look back and I'm so sorry, Minerva. I've missed you so much. Every time something went well—I got my first customer and the fabrics came in and I was able to read the order sheet—I thought of you, how proud you'd be. I wished you were here with me so many times, but I left you."

"Shh, it's all right, my dear girl," she said softly, crushing Abigail in her arms. "I'm so proud of everything you've accomplished. I love you, Abigail."

She let those words sink in, glorying in them. "I love you, too. I want you to stay. I've got two rooms in the back. We can say you're renting the other one and—"

That was as far as she got because Minerva kissed her and finally, after months of longing and wishing and, yes, *hoping*, Abigail suddenly had everything she ever wanted. She had control over her life, a livelihood and now—this. Love and acceptance and hope for happiness in the future.

"Let me love on you," Minerva whispered against her lips. "For the rest of our lives."

Abigail pulled away and hurried to the door of the shop.

"Abigail?" Minerva said, suddenly sounding nervous.

But Abigail just threw the bolt and drew the drapes to block out the sun. "The rest of our lives starts now, doesn't it?"

Minerva's face lit up with the widest smile Abigail had ever seen. "I do believe it does."

Abigail went to her, leading her back to the bedroom. "Welcome home, Minerva."

"Home," Minerva whispered against her neck, "is wherever you are."

Epilogue

One year later…

When Minerva got home from school that afternoon, Abigail said, "We had a letter," from where she was working on a scandalous red dress with crystals stitched into the bodice. Designed to catch the eye, that dress was—and in Madame Marsden's signature color.

The contrast between the madam's dress and Abigail's never failed to take Minerva's breath away. Today Abigail's dress was a golden yellow. The sleeves came down over her elbows and the neckline came a few inches below her chin. It was simply made—and perfectly respectable for a woman of business—but somehow its simplicity made it even more beautiful. Abigail always, *always* caught Minerva's eye. After a year, that hadn't changed and Minerva prayed it never would.

What had changed was Abigail's wardrobe. The girl wore dresses in golds and oranges and pinks and blues and greens now—almost every color in the rainbow.

Except black. She never wore black.

"Oh?" Since the shop was currently empty, Minerva kissed Abigail quickly before she hurried to the counter, the green cotton of her skirt swishing around her ankles. "I paid Mistress back already," she joked. It had taken the better part of the year, since Minerva refused to let Abigail use her own money for it. She'd tutored soiled doves, former slaves and newly minted millionaires who didn't want to sound uneducated anymore. Virginia City was awash in silver and Minerva had earned hers.

"It's not from Mistress. It's from Sadie."

"Oh?" Sadie was a Jewel—Miss Sapphire Bleu— back at the brothel in Brimstone. Minerva picked up the letter and carried it over to Abigail. "What news?"

Abigail laughed as she pinned a seam on the scandalous dress, lowering the bodice even more. "You could read it yourself, you know."

"I know. But I like to listen to you read, dear."

The year had been something Minerva had never allowed herself to dream of. She and Abigail had settled in together. To the rest of Virginia City, Minerva was a prickly schoolteacher renting a room from the dressmaker. But when Abigail locked the door at night, they became an old married couple, sharing laughter and love—so much love. More love than Minerva had thought she was capable of.

She glanced at the watch fob pinned to her green day dress. Abigail had sewn it for her little over a month ago and, as usual, Minerva felt glamorous in it. It was fitted to her waist and flared gently at her hips and it had a row of tiny mother-of-pearl buttons down the front and a draping of darker green around the waist. Perhaps it was too fine a dress for a schoolteacher, but she didn't care.

And when people asked her where she'd gotten the dress—or any of the dozen other dresses Abigail had stitched for her—Minerva always said the same thing.

225

White's. It's the only place for dresses.

Drat. Another hour until they could lock the door and Abigail could undo the tiny buttons on this dress and Minerva could unlace Abigail's corset…

"She's getting married," Abigail said around a mouthful of pins.

"She is? That's wonderful news." Any time a soiled dove could move on from a brothel was a thing to be celebrated. "To whom?"

Abigail lifted an eyebrow. "You'll never guess."

Minerva couldn't wait. She scanned the letter and then looked up at Abigail in shock. "Didn't you say that she liked…"

Abigail smiled knowingly. "I did."

"And she's marrying…*him*? Of all the men in that town?"

"She is."

Minerva stared at the name written in Sadie's neat hand in total surprise. Never in her nearly thirty years would she have guessed that Judge Gerard Hobson would marry a whore.

But then, no one would have ever guessed that Minerva would be all but married to one, either. So…

"Stranger things have happened," Abigail said, setting her pins down and pulling Minerva behind a dressing screen.

Hidden from view, Minerva lost herself in Abigail's kisses. "Can you close up early?" she asked against Abigail's lips. Because she didn't think she could wait another hour for this woman.

Abigail headed to the front door, throwing a knowing look back over her shoulder at Minerva.

Stranger things, indeed.

About the Author

Thanks so much for reading this *Jeweled Ladies* story! Leaving an honest review or telling a friend what you thought is the best way to show the love for your friendly local author!

Who is Maggie Chase? Writer, reader, crafter—I've told a lot of different stories a lot of different ways as Sarah M. Anderson, but the Jeweled Ladies series marks my first foray into historical erotica. I passionately believe that every single person deserves their own happily-ever-after and my stories reflect that hope on the page.

Readers can find out more about Maggie any of the following ways:

Sign up for her newsletter:
http://bit.ly/maggiechasenews

Visit her website:
http://www.maggiechase.com

Check out her Tumblr:
http://themaggiechase.tumblr.com/

Maggie Chase

Follow on Twitter:
http://twitter.com/TheMaggieChase

Leave a review on Goodreads:
http://www.goodreads.com/maggie_chase

Get Amazon pre-order information:
www.amazon.com/author/maggiechase

Other Books by Maggie Chase

The Jeweled Ladies: The Mistress Series

His Topaz
Their Emerald
Her Ebony
His Sapphire
His Crown Jewel

The Jeweled Ladies: The Rogues Series

His Diamond
His Amethyst

Now Available from Maggie Chase

Judge Gerard Hobson has lost control of his life. When Miss Sapphire Bleu promises to do whatever he wants, can he control himself—or will he ruin them both?

Read on for an excerpt of
HIS SAPPHIRE
a Jeweled Ladies story

Judge Gerard Hobson stood in his office, looking out the narrow window that faced Main Street.

He couldn't remember the last time he'd slept. Two days ago? Maybe three. His eyes felt like someone had ground sand into them and his jaw wasn't much better. Everything about him was scratchy and irritable.

He had lost the election for mayor of Brimstone, Texas—again. That in and of itself grated, but in the months since the election, he'd forged ahead. There were other ways to assume power, after all. But then that upstart whelp of Isabelle's, Raymond Dupree, had been chosen as the representative for the constitutional convention in Austin, Texas. Gerard had convinced himself that losing the election wouldn't be that bad, if he got appointed to the convention.

But he hadn't even gotten that.

Where had he gone wrong? He was doing the right thing. He *always* did the right thing. He had attempted to impose order upon this lawless town of Brimstone. This was *his* town, for God's sake. His grandfather, a hellfire-and-damnation preacher, had founded this town ten miles away from Fort Adams to save the god-fearing people from the sins of soldiers.

But did that matter? No. Brimstone had willingly settled into degeneracy and rebuffed every single one of Gerard's efforts to lead them back towards a righteous path.

Why wouldn't people do what he told them to? His actions were moral. The law was on his side. He was a God-fearing man. People should have been begging for him to take control of this town and set it on the correct path.

But were they? No. Instead, at every available opportunity to make the righteous choice, the people of this hellhole repeatedly chose that sinner, Raymond Dupree. They chose the brothels and the saloons over path of moral righteousness. They chose sin and violence.

Just like Isabelle had chosen Leopold Dupree all those years ago. All because Gerard had made a mistake and shown her what he really was. The last mistake he'd made.

Or so he'd thought.

But now this. He glanced back at the newspaper on his desk. It was a vile broadsheet—normally filled with murderers and crime and innuendo. But today took the cake.

"Judge Hobson rumored to be suspect in whore's disappearance."

230

No doubt, this was the work of his enemies. Dupree's man, Hank O'Shea—he was probably behind this ridiculously fabricated story. Wasn't it bad enough that Dupree was a living reminder of his failures? That Dupree beat him every time they came up against each other in an election? Did the impudent pup have to completely ruin Gerard's reputation?

The darkness within Gerard rose up and this time, he felt powerless to hold it at bay. His fingers clenched into fists and he struggled to hang onto his control. But he was failing. He just wanted to hit someone. He had spent years mastering his darkness—years of living by strict moral code that kept him far from sin—and where it gotten him?

"Judge Hobson rumored to be suspect in whore's disappearance."

The article was full of unsubstantiated innuendo. Four years ago, a prostitute from Beantown—over thirty miles north of Brimstone—had been dumped a few miles outside of town, her body cut to ribbons. The story said she was found with a silk necktie in her mouth and had made libelous claims that it was the same kind of necktie that he wore.

The darkness in him—it could have done that to a girl. That was why he had to keep it under control.

He hadn't killed that girl. Hell, he hadn't even been near a woman in years. Decades. Not since Isabelle. It was too risky.

He despised Raymond Dupree and his man, Hank O'Shea—but they were right about Gerard. He was dangerous. He always had been. He had recognized that early.

He scrubbed a hand over his face. He was so, *so*

tired. Tired of telling people what they should be doing and tired of them ignoring him. He was tired of losing to Dupree and tired of playing this cat and mouse game with O'Shea.

"Titus!" he called out.

Titus stuck his bull head through the office door. "Yes, Judge?"

For one brief second, Gerard mourned the fact that he had not been able to move Hank O'Shea away from Dupree. Titus served a purpose, but he didn't have any brains to speak of. Gerard appreciated that the man did what he was told, when he was told to do it, but he would never be anything more than a blunt instrument. "I need you to bring someone to me."

He couldn't push back against the darkness. Not anymore.

"An arrest?" Titus fancied himself a deputy.

Gerard shook his head. This would be outside of the law.

Titus' face sank into disappointment, rather like a hound dog that was kept on a leash. "Who?"

Gerard turned his attention back out to the narrow window. He was going to burn in hell for this. "Bring me Mistress."

Made in the USA
Coppell, TX
01 June 2021